The Crossroads
Just Before the Light

Brandon Michaels

The Crossroads Just Before the Light

First Printing

@AuthorBMichaels

authorbrandonmichaels@gmail.com

This is a work of fiction. Names, characters, businesses, places, events, locales, and incidents are either the products of the author's imagination or used in a fictitious manner. Any resemblance to actual persons, living or dead, or actual events is purely coincidental.

Trigger Warning

This book contains themes and descriptions of addiction, abuse, trauma, suicide, and violence, which may be distressing to some readers. Please take care when reading and prioritize your well-being.

If you or someone you know is struggling, consider reaching out for support:

National Suicide Prevention Lifeline (U.S.): 1-800-273-TALK (8255) or visit https://suicidepreventionlifeline.org

Crisis Text Line: Text HOME to 741741 (U.S., U.K., and Canada)

Substance Abuse and Mental Health Services Administration (SAMHSA) Helpline: 1-800-662-HELP (4357) or visit https://www.samhsa.gov

National Helpline (U.K.): Call 116 123 (Samaritans) or visit https://www.samaritans.org

Lifeline Australia: Call 13 11 14 or visit https://www.lifeline.org.au

Alcoholics Anonymous (AA): Visit https://www.aa.org for global resources

Narcotics Anonymous (NA): Visit https://www.na.org for global resources

You are not alone, and help is available.

Dedication

To those who have endured the unbearable weight of loss and addiction—this is for you. May you find strength in your struggle and know that hope, however distant, still flickers.

To those who stand in the shadows, offering love and support—family, friends, counselors, and healers—your quiet resilience and compassion are lifelines in the darkest of times.

And to all who seek redemption, even when it feels out of reach—never stop searching for the light.

Table of Contents

Prologue

Light is still possible even in the darkest moments when life feels hopeless and overwhelming. It may not be easy to see and seem impossible, but hope can be found even in the bleakest times. Life's most demanding challenges can cloud our vision, making it difficult to believe that joy still exists, but that doesn't mean it's gone. Though the road may be long and painful, there is strength in holding on and looking for good in even the smallest moments.

God's love and support are always there, especially when we need them most. In times of deep pain and despair, trusting in Him can remind us that we are never truly alone. Faith doesn't remove our struggles but gives us the strength to endure them, knowing that a higher power holds us. Even when it feels like we can't carry the weight of our burdens, God offers us His presence and the promise of better days ahead.

It takes great courage to find hope amid suffering; sometimes, that hope is faint. But even in our weakest moments, blessings await us if we seek them out. Life's challenges, though painful, can become growth opportunities. With resilience, faith, and perseverance, we can move toward a brighter future, trusting that God will guide us through.

Though the road may be hard, remember that you are never alone. There is light, even when it's hard to see, and together with God, we can find the strength to carry on.

November 23rd, 1998

It was a cold November morning, and the wind seeped through Alex's thin jacket, sending a shiver down his spine. The sky was heavy, overcast gray, with clouds hanging low as if pressing down on the quiet suburban streets. The air was damp, filled with the smell of wet leaves clinging to the sidewalk, remnants of the trees now stripped bare. The wind was sharp, whispering through the branches, carrying a chill that nipped at Alex's ears and nose.

Alex, just eight years old, walked alone down the familiar path to school. The pavement beneath his feet was slick with moisture, and his shoes scuffed against the ground with each reluctant step. The school was only three blocks from his house, but today, like every day, it felt much farther. His small breath puffed out in clouds of vapor, the only warmth in the cold stillness of the morning.

When he was one block away, his heart sank. In the distance, he saw them—the two older boys, their figures looming larger as they approached. They had been tormenting him for days, calling him names and shoving him between them like a ragdoll. Their laughter, harsh and cruel, carried through the cold air as they spotted him.

Alex's instinct took over. Without thinking, he turned on his heels and ran, his small legs pumping against the cold resistance of the wind. But he was too slow. His breath came in short, frantic bursts as he heard their footsteps pound closer behind him. It didn't take long before they were on him.

The larger boy grabbed Alex's shoulder, yanking him back with such force that Alex stumbled, losing his balance. Before he could react, the first shove came—hard, sending him reeling into the other boy. They laughed as they tossed him between them like a toy, the wet pavement slick beneath his feet, making it impossible to stand steady.

Then, the larger boy's fist connected with Alex's face for the first time. The impact was sharp and sudden, like a crack of thunder in the still morning air. Alex's lip split open, and he tasted the metallic tang of blood as it dripped down his chin. He fell to the ground, the cold cement biting into his palms as he landed hard. Tears welled up in his eyes before he could stop them, hot and stinging against his cold cheeks.

He didn't want to cry. He never wanted to give them the satisfaction. But the pain was too much, and the tears came anyway, streaming down his face as the boys towered over him.

The larger boy sneered, a cruel glint in his eyes. Without warning, he kicked Alex in the side, the force knocking the wind out of him. Alex curled in on himself, clutching his ribs, his body trembling from pain and fear. The world around him blurred through the haze of his tears. He could hear the boys laughing above him, their breath visible in the chilly air, as they spat on him, their loogies hitting his face and clothes with sickening wetness.

Lying there, bruised, bleeding, and broken, Alex wondered why it was always him. Why he was the one who had to endure this? The world around him felt distant and uncaring— just like the dark, empty sky above. All he could hear now was the fading echo of the boys' laughter as they walked away, leaving him alone on the cold ground.

December 8th, 1998

It was a crisp winter evening, the kind where the air was cold but not quite freezing. The sun had dipped below the horizon, leaving a soft orange glow fading into the deep blue sky. The porch light flickered on, casting a warm but lonely glow onto the small yard where eight-year-old Alex sat on the worn wooden steps, his knees pulled up to his chest. His breath formed little clouds in front of his face as he absentmindedly blew into the air, watching it disappear into the night.

Alex stared down at his scuffed sneakers, kicking at the chipped paint on the porch steps, his thoughts heavy with questions no one seemed willing to answer. He had repeatedly asked his momma, "Why doesn't Daddy want to spend time with me?" Her response was the same each time: "He's just busy, Alex. He works a lot." But deep down, Alex wasn't sure if he believed that anymore. The way his father avoided him and never asked about school or joined him in playing catch didn't feel like the actions of a man who was simply busy.

The night was growing colder, and the last remnants of daylight were fading quickly, leaving the sky dotted with faint stars. A distant wind rustled through the bare branches of the trees, sending a few stray leaves skittering across the driveway. Alex shivered and tucked his arms into his jacket, the cold biting his cheeks and fingers. The house behind him was quiet, only the faint hum of the TV inside drifting through the front door, which had been left slightly ajar.

Then, the familiar sound of tires crunching on the gravel driveway reached his ears. Alex's heart skipped a beat as he looked up, spotting the headlights of his father's old sedan pulling into the driveway. The car rolled to a stop, and the engine cut off, leaving an eerie stillness. For a moment, Alex held his breath, hoping, just maybe, this time would be different. He imagined his father stepping out of the car, smiling, asking how his day was, or inviting him inside to play a game.

But instead, the car door opened with a creak, and his father, tall and distant, stepped out, his face tired and worn from another long day of work. He didn't glance at Alex, and he didn't even seem to notice him sitting there on the porch. His father's shoulders were hunched, his jacket pulled tight against the cold as he trudged toward the front door. The gravel crunched under his boots, the only sound breaking the silence, and Alex's small heart sank deeper with each step his father took.

Without a word, his father disappeared into the house, letting the door swing shut behind him with a soft click. Alex stared after him, his chest tightening with a familiar ache that came from too many nights just like this one.

He wanted to go inside, ask his father if they could spend time together, and find out if something was wrong with him that made his father ignore him. But the weight of rejection kept him rooted to the porch. He stayed there, his small figure huddled against the cold, his mind swirling with unspoken questions and unhealed wounds. The world around him felt so much bigger and emptier at that moment as if he were a tiny speck in a vast, indifferent universe.

The night deepened, the stars twinkling faintly overhead, and Alex remained on the porch, sitting in the quiet loneliness that had become all too familiar. His father didn't come back out. And Alex knew he wouldn't.

December 25th, 1998

Christmas had always been a magical time for Alex. He loved how the world seemed to transform overnight, the houses lining the street adorned with twinkling lights, glowing reindeer on lawns, and wreaths hung on every door. The smell of pine filled the living room from the decorated tree, shimmering with ornaments that reflected the soft glow of the colored lights. It was a time that used to bring him joy—a day full of laughter, presents, and togetherness.

But this year, something was different. The house felt colder and darker despite the festive decorations. The tension in the air was as thick as the winter chill outside. His parents argued for weeks, their sharp voices cutting through the season's warmth like a cold wind. Sitting on the couch in his pajamas, Alex stared at the Christmas tree, its lights blinking lazily as if they had also lost their usual sparkle.

From the kitchen, his parents' voices began to rise again. At first, it was just a murmur, the kind of conversation Alex had gotten used to tuning out. But soon, the murmurs grew into harsh words, slicing through the Christmas morning quiet like a storm breaking over the horizon.

"You never listen to me!" his mother shouted, trembling angrily.

"I'm trying! You never give me a chance!" his father yelled, his frustration boiling over.

Alex's heart sank as the shouting intensified, bouncing off the walls of their small home, drowning out the cheerful sound of Christmas music playing softly from the living room radio. He had heard them argue before, but never like this—never so loud, so raw.

Clutching his new toy—a gift he had barely even looked at—Alex wanted nothing more than to disappear. The joy and excitement that usually filled him on Christmas morning had been replaced by a heavy sadness that weighed him down. He got up from the couch and retreated to his bedroom, where he crawled under his bed, curling up into a ball in the dim space. The darkness felt safe, like a shield from the world outside, muffling the sound of his parents' voices.

The minutes stretched on, each one slower than the last. His parents' argument continued forever, echoing in his ears. Tears welled up in Alex's eyes as he pressed his hands over his ears, trying to block it all out. This wasn't how Christmas was supposed to be. He didn't want to feel this way—not today.

Finally, after what felt like hours, the shouting stopped. The house was eerily quiet now, except for the faint clock ticking in the hallway and the occasional creak of the floorboards as his parents moved around. Alex knew they had calmed down, but the damage had already been done. The festive spirit was gone, replaced by an empty sadness that sat heavy in his chest.

He crawled out from under the bed, wiping his eyes with the sleeve of his pajama shirt. The house was still adorned with Christmas decorations—the tree still stood, the lights still blinked, but to Alex, it all felt hollow now.

Christmas was his favorite day of the year, filled with joy and togetherness. But this time, all Alex felt was alone, standing in the middle of a room that had once felt so warm but now seemed colder than the winter outside.

February 14th, 1999

Valentine's Day had always been a day that Alex looked forward to, a bright spot in the cold, bleak stretch of winter. He imagined it filled with colorful cards, candy hearts, and maybe— just maybe—a smile or two from his classmates. Even though he was often the lonely kid, always sitting alone at lunch and walking home silently, today felt like it could be different. He clutched his stack of Valentine's cards tightly in his small hands as he walked to school, each card carefully chosen and signed, ready to share with his classmates.

The classroom was decked out with pink and red decorations—paper hearts hung from the ceiling, and cheerful messages of love and friendship were drawn on the chalkboard. The room buzzed with excitement as the other kids shuffled in, giggling and trading secret smiles, their backpacks heavy with Valentine's cards and small boxes of candy.

Alex sat at his desk, his heart beating faster with anticipation. He sat up straighter, glancing around the room, waiting for someone to come to his desk with a card just for him. Today, he thought, would be different. Today, he wouldn't be the kid no one noticed.

Alex's eyes sparkled with hope as the teacher called the students up one by one to distribute their Valentines. He watched his classmates walk around the room, smiling as they handed out cards. Bright, colorful envelopes piled up on the desks around him, and laughter filled the air like a melody he couldn't quite reach.

But with each passing moment, that hopeful light in Alex's eyes began to dim. His classmates walked by his desk one by one, chatting and laughing, but no one stopped. No one placed a card on his desk. Alex's fingers curled tightly around the cards he had brought, his fists crumpling the edges as he fought to keep the growing knot of sadness in his chest from rising to his throat.

By the time the last student passed him, the air in the room felt stifling. His desk was empty. There were no bright envelopes, candy, or kind words scribbled on a card, just the cold, hard surface staring back at him. Alex's heart felt heavy, like a cold winter wind had blown through it, leaving a hollow ache.

He could hear the other kids chatting, comparing their piles of cards, and laughing over silly notes. It all seemed to fade into the background, a distant hum as Alex sat there, trying to make himself invisible. He stared down at his stack of Valentines, still gripped tightly, cards meant for classmates who hadn't even thought of him.

He bit his lip, willing himself not to cry. But the sting of rejection was too strong, the loneliness too deep. It felt as if the room had shrunk, closing in around him, while everyone else moved on, their lives filled with warmth and connection that Alex couldn't touch.

The teacher's voice rang out, announcing the end of the Valentine exchange, but Alex barely heard it. All he could think about was the empty space in front of him, the cold feeling in his chest, and the sharp reminder that, once again, he was alone.

April 1st, 1999

Alex had woken up that morning with excitement bubbling in his chest. April Fool's Day was finally here, and he couldn't wait to join the fun. He had never been much of a prankster, but he thought things might be different this year. Maybe today, the other kids would let him in on their jokes. Perhaps he'd finally feel like he belonged.

The day started like any other. The schoolyard buzzed with energy, kids laughing and whispering about their pranks. Alex stood on the edge of the group, waiting for his chance to be part of it all. But as the morning went on, something changed. The playful excitement in the air began to feel heavy, like a storm gathering on the horizon.

It wasn't long before the pranks turned on him. First, a group of boys ran up to Alex, their grins wide and mischievous. Before he could even react, they dumped a bucket of cold water over his head, drenching him from head to toe. The icy shock made him gasp, and the boys' laughter surrounded him. His clothes clung to his skin, and his hair dripped water into his eyes, but the worst part was the laughter. It wasn't the lighthearted kind—this was sharp, mocking.

He tried to shake it off, telling himself it was just a joke, just part of the day. But as he sat down in his chair later in class, a loud "frrrrt" echoed through the room. Alex's face flushed bright red as he realized they had slipped a whoopee cushion under his seat. The class laughed, pointing and snickering as Alex sank deeper into his chair, wishing he could disappear.

Then came the silly string. During recess, more kids ganged up on him, spraying neon green and pink string into his hair until it was a sticky, tangled mess. It clung to his clothes and face, and he could barely see through the strands. The other kids giggled and ran off, leaving Alex alone in the schoolyard, his cheeks burning with shame.

He tried to fight back the tears, but they welled up in his eyes, threatening to spill over. The laughter from his classmates echoed in his ears, each giggle and snicker feeling like a sharp jab to his heart. He felt humiliated, a walking target for everyone else's amusement.

When the final bell rang, Alex hurried out of school, his eyes cast down, hoping to avoid any more pranks. But as he walked home, his heart heavy and his clothes still sticky from the silly string, he noticed something ahead. A group of kids, those same classmates who had laughed at him all day, were crossing the street toward his house. He could see their grinning faces, and his stomach twisted with dread.

They were carrying something. As Alex got closer, he saw eggs. His breath caught in his throat. He knew they were up to no good. Panic surged through him, and he broke into a run, his heart pounding. But it was too late.

The kids caught up to him quickly. The first egg hit him square in the back, the cold yolk splattering across his shirt. Then came another and another. Each egg hit him with a sickening smack, cracking open and leaving trails of yellow slime dripping down his body. The laughter of the other kids was deafening, a cruel chorus that rang in his ears as they pelted him over and over until he was covered in egg yolk and slime, humiliated and broken.

Alex couldn't hold back the tears any longer. He ran the rest of the way home, his vision blurred with tears, his body trembling from the cold and the shame. The sticky, slimy mess clung to his skin, but what hurt the most was the cruelty—the way they had singled him out, making him the butt of their jokes.

When he reached his front door, his tears were flowing freely. He fumbled with the doorknob, wanting nothing more than to crawl into his room, away from laughter and pain.

As he passed through the house to his room, his mother called out to him, but Alex kept going to his room, not answering her. Alex just wanted to be alone and forget about what had just happened.

July 4th, 1999

The Fourth of July had always been one of Alex's favorite days. For weeks, he looked forward to the neighborhood block party, an afternoon filled with laughter, the smell of burgers on the grill, games with friends, and the grand finale of fireworks lighting up the night sky. For the last three years, it had been the highlight of his summer, a day when everything felt perfect when the world seemed a little brighter.

This year, the sun hung high in the sky, casting golden light over the rows of houses, their porches decorated with red, white, and blue streamers. The block was buzzing with activity— neighbors chatting, kids running through sprinklers, and the clatter of dishes being set on picnic tables. With a grin on his face, Alex played tag with a few friends, darting between the parked cars and lawn chairs, his heart pounding excitedly. But as he raced past the driveway, his fun suddenly stopped.

A group of older kids, boys he recognized from school, approached him with smirks plastered across their faces. The day's joy vanished instantly, replaced by a creeping sense of dread. Alex's stomach tightened as they closed in on him, their eyes cold and predatory. The laughter of his friends faded into the background as these older boys began their assault.

"Look who it is, the little crybaby," one of them sneered, stepping forward. Before Alex could even think of running, a fist slammed into his stomach, knocking the wind out. The sharp pain rippled through his small frame, and he doubled over, gasping for air.

Another boy shoved him, and Alex stumbled backward, his legs giving out beneath him as he fell hard onto the ground. The hot pavement scraped against his skin, but the pain in his body was nothing compared to the humiliation that came next. The older boys kicked him while he was down, their laughter echoing around him as he curled into himself, trying to protect his face.

The other kids, his friends—the ones he had just been playing with—stood frozen, watching silently. None of them stepped in. None of them came to his defense. Alex felt the sting of their betrayal as sharply as the kicks landing against his ribs.

His heart raced in panic, his body trembling, and then it happened—he urinated on himself. The warmth spread across his legs, and he felt the shame crash over him in waves, drowning out everything else. His face burned with humiliation, his tears mixing with the dirt on his cheeks. He wanted to disappear, to melt into the ground so no one could see him like this.

The beating continued, the older kids laughing and calling him names—"Weak," "Pathetic," "Baby." The words cut deeper than the punches, leaving scars that wouldn't heal. Alex squeezed his eyes shut, trying to block it all out, praying for it to stop.

Then, finally, his mother's voice rang out, sharp and angry, cutting through the chaos.

"Get away from him!" she screamed, rushing across the yard. The boys scattered, taking off in a run as soon as they saw her. Alex lay on the ground, his body aching, his face streaked with tears and dirt. His mom knelt beside him, her hands shaking as she touched his arm gently, checking him for injuries.

"Alex, honey, are you okay?" she asked, her voice soft now but filled with worry.

He didn't answer. He couldn't. The words were stuck in his throat, buried beneath the shame and fear. He just nodded weakly as she helped him to his feet.

As they made their way toward the house, Alex glanced back toward the party, where people were still laughing and celebrating as if nothing had happened. But his eyes landed on his father, standing by the porch, arms crossed. His father wasn't rushing toward him. He wasn't asking if Alex was okay.

Instead, his father just stood there, shaking his head in disappointment.

That look, his father's silent, disapproving stare, hit Alex harder than any punches. It felt like all the air had been sucked out of his lungs, leaving him hollow. Tears streamed down his face, but he quickly wiped them away, hoping his father didn't see.

Inside the house, his mom cleaned him up, her hands gentle as she wiped away the dirt and bandaged his scrapes. But no matter how much she tried to comfort him, that day's weight stayed with Alex, pressing down on him like a shadow that wouldn't lift.

Outside, the fireworks would go on, but for Alex, the sparkle and excitement of the Fourth of July had been extinguished.

July 12th, 1999

Alex had counted the days to his ninth birthday party for what felt like forever. The backyard was decorated with bright streamers, balloons swaying in the gentle summer breeze, and a giant banner that read "Happy Birthday Alex!" hung above the picnic table. His mom had made his favorite cake—a chocolate one with blue frosting and a rocket ship on top—and the smell of grilling burgers filled the air. Everything was set for what was supposed to be a perfect day.

He had handed out invitations at school weeks ago, inviting all his classmates and friends. In his mind, he imagined a day filled with laughter, games, and presents. But as the sun rose higher in the sky, something felt off. The yard was empty, save for his parents, who were busy setting things up. The table was still bare, with no plates filled with cake and no presents stacked high. Alex sat on the porch, fidgeting with the party hat his mom had made him wear, his eyes glued to the street, waiting for the first guest to arrive.

Minutes turned into hours, and still, no one showed up. His parents tried to keep up the excitement. His mom smiled reassuringly, patting him on the back. "They're probably just running a little late, sweetheart," she said, though Alex could hear the strain in her voice. His dad was quieter, flipping burgers on the grill but occasionally glancing toward the empty street, his lips pressed into a thin line.

But Alex knew. He had seen them earlier—his classmates, the same kids he had invited, walking down the street, laughing and talking as they passed his house without glancing in his direction. They weren't coming. No one was.

The once bright and festive decorations now felt like a mockery. The balloons seemed to droop under his disappointment, the vibrant colors dull in his eyes. The cake, still perfectly untouched on the table, looked too big, too grand for the small, empty gathering that had become his birthday party. Even the birds chirping overhead felt too cheerful for what was happening inside Alex's heart.

His parents tried their best. They sat with him, sang Happy Birthday with forced smiles, and cut the cake, but the laughter disappeared. Alex took a bite of cake, but it tasted like sand in his mouth. He didn't want cake. He didn't want to play games or open presents. All he wanted was to go back in time, to cancel the party before this feeling of rejection and loneliness had a chance to set in.

As the afternoon wore on, Alex retreated to his room, away from the reminders of what could have been. The colorful streamers, the untouched gifts, and the now half-eaten cake all felt like reminders of a day that had turned into one of the worst in his young life.

September 21st, 1999

Alex had always prided himself on being a good student. He wasn't the fastest runner or the strongest kid, but he was brilliant, always turning in his homework on time and listening to his teachers. He preferred books over sports; while some kids teased him, he didn't mind. He liked the certainty of following the rules, knowing that things would go smoothly if he did everything right. But that day at recess, everything changed.

It was a relaxed autumn afternoon when the breeze carried the first hints of fall. The playground was alive with children laughing and shouting, their sneakers pounding on the pavement as they ran and played. Alex, trying to fit in, joined a game of tag, his heart racing as he weaved in and out of the kids chasing him. For a moment, he forgot about the teasing, about how out of place he usually felt. He was just a kid, running and laughing until everything went wrong.

As Alex rounded the corner near the swings, he didn't notice the boy sticking out his leg in his path. It happened so fast. One second, Alex was running full speed, and the next, his foot caught on something, and he was sent flying forward. Time seemed to slow as he hit the ground hard, the rough asphalt scraping his palms and knees. The laughter of his classmates rang out, sharp and cruel, as they pointed and snickered at him lying there, dazed and confused.

But the pain in his scraped hands was nothing compared to his knee's sharp, searing sensation. Alex tried to get up, but his leg buckled beneath him, the pain shooting up through his body like fire. He gasped, his vision blurring as he looked down at his leg, his breath catching in his throat.

His pants were soaked in blood. It spread quickly, staining the fabric a dark, angry red. Panic surged through him as he realized something was seriously wrong. His knee throbbed with every beat of his heart, and his stomach turned as he saw the jagged tear in his skin.

Teachers rushed over, their voices a blur as they tried to calm him down, but Alex couldn't focus on anything but the pain and the mocking laughter of his classmates that still echoed in his ears. Even as he lay there, bleeding and hurt, they laughed. Some of them whispered behind their hands; others smirked as they walked away, leaving Alex on the ground, his body trembling with pain and humiliation.

The trip to the hospital was a blur: his mom's worried face, the sterile smell of the emergency room, and the cold metal of the gurney beneath him. The doctors told him what he feared: he had not only lacerated his leg but torn his ACL. Surgery would be necessary, and the road to recovery would be long and difficult. But the physical pain, as unbearable as it was, wasn't the worst part.

When Alex returned to school weeks later, limping on crutches and trying to pretend everything was fine, the taunts picked up right where they left off. The other kids mocked him for his injury, calling him names and making jokes about how clumsy he was. They ridiculed him for needing help to get around and for being unable to keep up in gym class. Even when the physical wounds began to heal, the emotional scars lingered, deep and painful.

No matter what he did, Alex couldn't escape the ridicule. The laughter, the whispers, the feeling of being watched and judged—it all stayed with him, a constant reminder that no matter how hard he tried to be good, to follow the rules, it wasn't enough to protect him from the cruelty of the world around him.

October 31st, 1999

Halloween night was always one of Alex's favorite times of the year. He loved dressing up in costumes, collecting candy, and running through the crisp autumn air with the other kids in the neighborhood. But this year, things were different. His leg was still injured, and instead of joining his classmates outside, he sat alone by the window, watching the world pass him by.

From his perch at the window, Alex could see them—kids in colorful costumes, capes flowing, faces painted with masks and smiles. They raced from house to house, their laughter carrying on the breeze as they filled their bags with candy. Pumpkins flickered on front porches, casting a warm orange glow over the neighborhood, and the street was alive with excitement. It was the kind of night Alex used to be a part of that made him feel like a regular kid, just like everyone else. But not this year.

He sat there, his crutches propped up against the wall, his leg still bandaged and aching from the surgery. His Halloween costume hung untouched on the back of his door—a superhero cape his mom had helped him pick out weeks ago. He had imagined flying through the streets with his friends, cape billowing behind him, collecting candy until his bag was too heavy to carry. Instead, he was stuck inside, his heart heavy as he watched from the sidelines.

The glow of the streetlights and the chatter of trick-or-treaters filled the air, but inside the house, it was quiet and too calm. His parents had tried to cheer him up earlier with extra candy and a Halloween movie, but it wasn't the same. No amount of candy or comforting words could make up for the feeling of being left out.

Alex rested his forehead against the cool window glass, watching as group after group of kids passed by, their faces lit up with excitement, their bags overflowing with treats. They didn't know what it was like to be stuck inside, watching life go on without them. They didn't know how hard it was for him to see them run and laugh while he was left behind, his leg reminding him of how different things had become since the accident.

He wanted to be out there with them. He wanted to be part of the fun, to forget, even for a little while, that his leg was hurt and that he couldn't run like he used to. But he knew better. His body wouldn't let him.

Eventually, laughter and footsteps outside grew quieter as the night wore on, and Alex knew it was time for bed. His parents tucked him in, trying to reassure him with smiles that didn't quite reach their eyes. They knew how much this night meant to him.

As he lay in the darkness of his room, the weight of the day pressed down on him. He missed the days when he could run and play, when Halloween was about more than just watching from the window. Everything had felt harder since the accident—

school, friendships, even simple things like walking. And now, Halloween had been added to the growing list of things taken from him.

Tears welled in Alex's eyes as he pulled the blankets up to his chin, trying to push the sadness away. But it was too much. The loneliness and longing to be outside with everyone else were more than he could hold in. Silent sobs shook his body as he cried himself to sleep, the sound of distant laughter from the street outside fading into the quiet of the night.

January 1st, 2000

The house was unnervingly quiet as Alex tiptoed down the hallway. The soft creak of the floorboards beneath his feet seemed louder in the stillness of the early morning. He tried to be as silent as possible—his parents were in their bedroom, and the last thing he wanted was to wake them. Something about the way they had acted the night before made him uneasy. He had never seen them like that before.

It had been New Year's Eve, a night that should have been filled with celebration, the promise of a new beginning. But instead of joy, the house had been filled with shouting, slurred words, and the clinking of too many bottles. Alex had hidden away in his room, trying to block out the noise, pretending everything was fine. But he knew something was wrong. Even now, with the house still and dark, the unsettling feeling lingered in his chest.

He stopped outside his parents' bedroom door, his small hand hovering over the doorknob. His stomach twisted with a strange dread, but he couldn't help himself. He had to see if they were okay. Slowly, he pushed the door open just a crack, peering inside. His heart dropped.

The room smelled faintly of alcohol, stale and sour in the cool air. Half-dressed, his parents sprawled out on the bed, the sheets tangled around their legs. Empty bottles littered the floor by the nightstand, and their faces were slack, their bodies limp with sleep. They were passed out, unmoving, oblivious to the world around them. Alex stared at them, a lump forming in his throat as embarrassment and shame swelled inside him.

He had never seen them like this before—so vulnerable, so...broken. His mom's hair was messy, her clothes disheveled, and his dad's shirt hung open, exposing his chest. The sight burned Alex's face with an emotion he couldn't fully name. He knew they were drunk. He had seen people drink before, but never his parents like this. They had always been in control, but now, they looked helpless, and it frightened him.

Alex felt a strange, overwhelming urge to close the door, to shut out the sight of his parents like that. He didn't want to see them like this; he wanted to remember them as the strong, dependable adults they were supposed to be. But the image was already burned into his mind.

He quietly shut the door and turned away, his chest tight as he went downstairs. Each step felt heavier than the last, the weight of what he had seen pressing down on him. He didn't know what to do, didn't know how to process the strange mix of emotions swirling inside him. All he knew was that he felt so alone and couldn't explain why.

In the dim light of the kitchen, Alex sat down at the table, his fingers tracing the worn wood of the surface. He wanted to cry, but the tears wouldn't come. Instead, he just sat there, staring at the shadows on the wall, the house's silence surrounding him like a blanket he couldn't shake off. He felt small, vulnerable, and scared.

He had always thought his parents were invincible and would always be the ones to take care of him. But now, seeing them like this—passed out, unaware of the world around them—made him feel more lost than ever. He didn't understand why, but something about it filled him with a deep, gnawing fear. It wasn't just the sight of them; it was the realization that the people he depended on weren't as strong as he had thought.

Sitting there in the stillness of the early morning, Alex felt the weight of that truth settle over him. He didn't know what to do. He didn't know how to make sense of the fear and sadness gnawing at him. All he knew was that something had changed, and he wasn't sure things would ever feel the same again.

April 14th, 2000

Alex was only nine, but he had learned to recognize the signs. He could see the way his mom's eyes would darken with sadness, how she'd wince when his dad raised his voice. The air in the house had become tense, like a storm on the verge of breaking. His parents had been fighting more often, and Alex didn't understand all the reasons, but he knew it wasn't good. The arguments were louder and angrier and seemed to last longer each time. One night, it was worse than usual.

Alex had been in his room, the soft glow of his bedside lamp barely cutting through the darkness as he lay on his bed, trying to focus on the book in his hands. But the muffled sound of voices from the kitchen downstairs kept pulling him out of the story. His mom's voice, usually so calm, was strained, rising and falling like she was holding back tears. His dad's voice, on the other hand, was rough and slurred; he was drunk again. Alex could tell just by the way his dad's words fumbled together.

The argument grew louder, angrier. Dishes clattered, and a chair scraped harshly across the floor. Alex's heart raced. He had heard them fight before, but this time, something felt different. An edge in his dad's voice sent a shiver down Alex's spine, a kind of anger that was sharper than usual. His mom was pleading now, her words trembling, but Alex couldn't understand what she was saying. All he knew was that it wasn't good.

Suddenly, he heard heavy footsteps coming up the stairs. The sound was like thunder in the house's stillness, and Alex's body froze. His stomach twisted in knots, fear gripping him tightly as he realized his dad was coming toward his room.

He quickly slid under the covers, pulling the blanket over his head as if that could make him invisible. His body trembled as he curled up, trying to make himself as small as possible, praying his dad wouldn't come in. But the footsteps stopped right outside his door.

The door swung open with a creak, and his dad stormed in. Alex could hear the heavy breathing and smell the alcohol on his breath, even from beneath the covers. His dad's voice was a snarl, filled with anger that Alex didn't understand.

"Why do you always have to be such a little shit?" his dad yelled, the words cutting through the air like a slap. Alex squeezed his eyes tighter, willing himself not to cry or move. His heart pounded in his chest, and every muscle in his body was tense with fear. He didn't dare speak, didn't dare move, hoping that if he stayed still enough, his dad might leave.

The yelling continued, each word hitting Alex like a physical blow. The tears came, despite his efforts to hold them back, and they soaked into his pillow as he cowered under the covers. He felt powerless, trapped, as his dad's words rained down on him, filled with a rage that Alex couldn't understand.

Finally, after what felt like hours but was probably only minutes, his dad turned and left the room. Alex didn't move or breathe until he heard the slam of the front door and the screech of tires as his dad drove away into the night.

The house was quiet again, but the silence was heavy and oppressive. Alex lay there, still trembling, still hiding under the covers, even though his dad was gone. His heart ached with a mixture of fear, sadness, and confusion. He didn't understand why this was happening, why his dad seemed so angry, or why his mom looked so sad. All he knew was that something was deeply wrong, and no matter how hard he tried, he couldn't make it go away.

The night stretched on, and eventually, exhaustion took over. Alex drifted off to sleep, his cheeks still wet with tears; he curled up under the blankets as if they could shield him from the world outside.

June 28th, 2000

The car ride to the rehab center was quiet, and the engine's hum was the only sound as Alex stared out the window, his mind swirling with uncertainty. It had been months since he'd last seen his dad, months of awkward silences at home and whispered conversations between his mom and relatives. Now, as the car turned onto the long driveway of the rehab facility, Alex's stomach twisted with a mixture of nervousness and hope. He didn't know what to expect. He wasn't even sure if he'd recognize his dad, the man who had disappeared into the haze of anger and alcohol so long ago.

The building was large and plain, set back from the road with tall trees surrounding it, their leaves rustling gently in the warm summer breeze. Alex and his mom walked through the front doors, the sterile smell of disinfectant and the soft buzz of fluorescent lights greeting them as they entered. The air felt different here, calmer, more controlled. It starkly contrasted with the chaos that had defined their home for so long.

They were greeted by a counselor, a kind-faced woman who smiled warmly at Alex before ushering them into a small office. The room was simple, with a few chairs and a desk, but it felt safe. The counselor explained how his dad was doing and how he was progressing in his recovery. As she spoke, Alex felt a slight weight lift from his chest. His dad was getting better. He was making progress. Maybe things really could change.

After the meeting, they walked down a long, quiet hallway, their footsteps echoing softly off the walls. Alex's heart raced as they approached a door at the end of the corridor. His dad was behind that door, and for the first time in what felt like forever, Alex wasn't sure if he was ready to see him. What if his dad hadn't changed? What if things were still the same?

But when the door opened, Alex saw a man sitting there, his dad, but somehow different. He looked thinner and tired, but his eyes were clearer than Alex remembered, and when he smiled, it didn't seem forced. His dad stood up slowly, and for a moment, there was an awkward silence as they looked at each other. Then, with a hesitant step forward, his dad pulled Alex into a gentle hug.

"Hey, buddy," his dad said, his voice soft but steady.

"Hey, Dad," Alex replied, his heart pounding.

They sat down together, Alex's mom stepping back to let them have time alone. The initial awkwardness slowly melted away as they began to talk. At first, the conversation was light, with minor updates about the school, what Alex had been doing over the summer, and what his dad had been working on in rehab. But as the minutes passed, Alex found himself surprised. His dad was actually...funny. The man who once seemed distant and angry now cracked jokes and smiled in a way Alex hadn't seen in years.

They talked for a long time about everything and nothing at once. His dad explained to him what had happened, how he had been what people called a "functioning alcoholic," someone who could appear to have it all together on the outside while falling apart on the inside. He admitted that he hadn't been there for Alex as he should have been but was working hard to change that.

"I'm going to be more available to you, Alex," his dad said, his voice sincere. "I know I've made many mistakes, but I want to improve for you, for us."

Alex didn't say much, but he nodded, feeling a mix of emotions, relief, hope, and a tiny flicker of something he hadn't felt in a long time: trust. For the first time in what seemed like forever, his dad was talking to him, really talking, not just yelling or brushing him off. It was different. It felt real.

As the visit ended, Alex stood up, feeling lighter than he had in months. There was still a long way to go; he knew that. But for the first time, he believed things could improve. Maybe his dad was changing.

Before they left, his dad gave him another hug, tighter this time, and Alex hugged him back without hesitation. As they walked back down the hallway, out into the warm afternoon sun, Alex glanced over his shoulder at the rehab center. It wasn't much to look at, but it was where his dad started to find himself again. And that gave Alex hope.

July 12th, 2000

Alex had been counting the days to his 10th birthday with excitement and hope. This year was supposed to be different. His dad had been doing better since getting out of rehab—more present, more involved. Alex had imagined them celebrating together, maybe tossing a ball in the yard or sharing laughs over cake. But as the day wore on, the weight of disappointment settled in.

The backyard was decorated with colorful streamers and balloons, the smell of hamburgers and hot dogs grilling in the air, but something was missing. His dad wasn't there. He was supposed to be home by now, supposed to join in the celebration, but the minutes ticked by, and there was no sign of him. Alex sat at the picnic table, trying to focus on the party and the friends who had shown up, but his eyes drifted toward the driveway, waiting for his father's car to pull in.

He blew out the candles on his cake as everyone sang Happy Birthday, but his heart wasn't in it. He tried to smile and pretend everything was fine, but his dad's absence loomed over the day like a dark cloud. His friends' laughter and chatter felt distant and muted. All he could think about was the space at the table, the one where his father should have been sitting.

Alex's hope faded as the hours passed, and the sun began to dip lower in the sky. His dad still hadn't come home. He tried to brush it off, telling himself that maybe work had run late, that maybe his dad would show up soon, but deep down, he knew the truth. His dad wasn't coming. Not today.

The rest of the day dragged on, but Alex could barely enjoy it. His mind was elsewhere, filled with questions he was too afraid to ask. Why did his dad always seem to choose work over him? Why did it feel like he wasn't a priority despite all the promises?

Later that evening, as the party wound down and the guests left, Alex sat alone in his room, staring at the birthday presents piled on the floor. He didn't feel like opening them. He didn't feel like celebrating anymore. His dad had been sober for months now, and Alex had thought things were getting better, but now he realized that it wasn't just the drugs and alcohol that had kept his dad away. It was something more, something more complicated.

His dad's work had always come first. Even before rehab, Alex had known that. He had gotten used to the long nights, the missed dinners, the broken promises. But on his birthday, as he sat alone in the quiet of his room, it became painfully clear just how much less of a priority he was in his father's life. It wasn't just the drinking or the drugs that had kept his dad away. It was everything: his work, responsibilities, and need to be elsewhere.

Alex hugged his knees to his chest, staring out the window at the fading light. He had spent months hoping that things would be different, that his dad would change, but today felt like a cruel reminder that some things would never change. Sure, his dad had made progress, but it wasn't enough for Alex.

That night, as he lay in bed, Alex couldn't shake the sadness that had settled deep inside him. His 10th birthday had come and gone, but the one thing he had wanted more than anything—a few hours with his dad—had slipped through his fingers. He didn't cry. He just stared up at the ceiling, feeling a little more grown-up than he had that morning, a little more aware of the distance between him and his father.

November 23rd, 2000

Thanksgiving had always been one of Alex's favorite days. It wasn't just about the food or the holiday itself—it was the one time of year when he and his dad would bond over making the turkey. Standing side by side in the kitchen, seasoning the bird, laughing over little mistakes, and creating something together had become their tradition. For a few hours, it felt like they were connected. But this year was different.

His dad wasn't coming home. Work had called him into the city, and even though Alex had tried to hide his disappointment when his dad told him, the hurt had settled deep. He had spent days hoping that maybe his dad would change his mind, that he'd surprise him and come home in time for the holiday. But Thanksgiving morning came, and the house felt emptier than ever.

Once filled with laughter and the smell of roasting turkey, the kitchen was now a quiet space where his mom moved about, trying to make the best of the day. Alex stayed out of the way, his heart heavy with sadness he couldn't shake. Without his dad there, everything felt wrong.

He sat at the table, picking at his food as the meal began. The turkey, usually a symbol of his and his dad's teamwork, sat on the table, but it was dry and flavorless. The traditional side dishes of mashed potatoes, stuffing, and cranberry sauce felt like tasteless remnants of something that should have been special. Alex couldn't bring himself to enjoy any of it. His dad's absence was a void that no amount of food could fill.

The tension simmered quietly between Alex and his mom. She tried to keep things cheerful, asking him how he liked the meal, trying to get him to talk about his day. But Alex could only give short, mumbled responses, his eyes downcast as he pushed the food around his plate.

Finally, it all boiled over. It started as a small comment from his mom about him not eating enough, but it quickly escalated. Alex snapped back, his frustration and sadness spilling out into sharp words. They argued—about nothing. The kind of argument that wasn't about what was said but about everything that had been building underneath. Alex felt a storm of emotions swirling inside him—anger at his dad for not being there, guilt for snapping at his mom, and sadness that Thanksgiving had become a hollow shell of what it once was.

By the time dinner was over, the table was still full of uneaten food, the atmosphere thick with tension. Alex couldn't stand it anymore. He pushed his chair back and stormed up to his room, leaving his mom in the kitchen without a word. His heart ached as he threw himself onto his bed, burying his face in his pillow.

Tears came quickly, and Alex cried alone in his room for the second time that year, overwhelmed by disappointment. He missed his dad. He missed the way Thanksgiving used to be when it was something they shared. But most of all, he hated how much things had changed no matter what; it seemed like his dad was always too far away, physically and emotionally.

As the night stretched, Alex cried until exhaustion took over, and he fell asleep, his pillow damp with tears. Thanksgiving, a day supposed to bring warmth and togetherness, had left him more alone than ever.

May 24th, 2001

The afternoon sun hung low in the sky as Alex walked home from school, his backpack slung over his shoulder. The day had been uneventful, but his mind was preoccupied with thoughts of homework and what he might do after dinner. He kept his head down, lost in his world when suddenly, he felt a presence behind him.

Before Alex could react, a fist slammed into his back, sending him stumbling forward. He barely had time to register what was happening before the bully—a boy from his school who had tormented him for months—grabbed him by the collar and punched him square in the face. The sharp, blinding pain of the impact hit him immediately, radiating through his skull as he fell to the ground.

Alex tried to get up, but the bully was relentless. A kick to his stomach knocked the wind out of him, leaving him gasping for air. Another punch landed on his arm, and Alex's vision blurred as he curled up on the ground, trying to protect himself. The blows kept coming, punches, kicks, until all he could do was lie there, helpless, his body wracked with pain.

The world seemed to slow down as the bully, satisfied with his handiwork, spat on the ground next to Alex and walked away, leaving him bruised, broken, and humiliated. Alex's nose throbbed, blood dripping onto the pavement, and every inch of his body ached from the beating. His hands shook as he tried to push himself up, but the pain was too much. He collapsed back onto the ground, tears stinging his eyes, not just from the physical pain but from the deep sense of humiliation that cut even more profound.

By the time he made it home, Alex's face was swollen, his clothes stained with blood. His father was waiting for him in the living room, and as soon as he saw Alex's injuries, his expression shifted from shock to anger.

"What the hell happened to you?" his father demanded, his voice rough.

Alex's throat tightened as he recounted the attack, his voice shaky and low. His father listened, but instead of the sympathy Alex had hoped for, his dad's face grew darker, his jaw clenched in frustration.

"You just let him beat you like that? You didn't fight back?" his father asked, his tone sharp.

"I—I was scared," Alex stammered, his eyes downcast. "I didn't want to get hurt worse."

His father's eyes narrowed, disappointment etched on his face. "You need to fight back, Alex. You can't let people push you around like that. You've got to be a man. Next time, you fight back. At least try."

Alex didn't respond, his chest tightening with fear and shame. He wanted to explain that he couldn't, that he was too afraid, that the thought of getting hit again terrified him. But the words stuck in his throat. His father's demand for toughness felt impossible—how was he supposed to be strong when all he wanted to do was avoid the pain?

"You need to toughen up," his father continued sternly. "You can't be scared forever."

Alex stood there, his body aching, his heart heavy. He wished he could be the person his father wanted him to be, but the fear was too overwhelming. He had seen what fighting back looked like—it looked like more punches, more kicks, more pain. He couldn't bear the thought of going through it again.

That night, as Alex lay in bed, his face still throbbing and his body bruised, his father's words echoed in his mind. "Be a man." But what did that even mean? Did being a man mean fighting, hurting, and risking getting hurt again? Or was there something wrong with him because he couldn't do it?

The fear stayed with him, gnawing at the edges of his thoughts as the pain from the attack slowly faded into the background. But the sense of shame, the feeling that he had failed his father and wasn't strong enough, clung to him long after the bruises had healed.

September 11th, 2001

The day seemed like any other. Alex was sitting in his fourth-grade classroom, tapping his pencil against the desk and half-listening to the teacher. A sunny morning usually made Alex daydream about recess or playing after school. But everything changed instantly when the teacher's voice faltered, and she was called out of the room. When she returned, her face was pale, her voice shaky as she tried to explain what had happened.

"There's been an attack on the World Trade Center," she said softly, but her words sent a ripple of shock through the room.

Alex's heart dropped. His father worked in the Trade Center. He could hear his classmates' murmur of confused and scared voices, but the noise felt distant. All Alex could think about was his dad. A cold, sick feeling settled in his stomach, and suddenly, the classroom walls seemed to close in around him. He couldn't focus on anything, and his mind raced with terrifying possibilities. Was his dad okay? Had he gotten out in time? The questions spun in his head like a storm he couldn't control.

The rest of the day passed in a blur. His teacher tried to continue the lesson, but Alex couldn't listen. He just sat there, staring blankly out the window, his eyes glazed with worry. His heart pounded in his chest, and no matter how hard he tried, he couldn't stop the fear from gnawing at him. The scenes he imagined were unbearable smoke, fire, chaos, and his father somewhere in the middle.

Alex raced home as fast as he could when the final bell rang. His mom was already in front of the TV, the news flashing images of the towers collapsing, debris everywhere, people running for their lives. Alex's stomach churned as he watched the footage, the smoke and destruction filling the screen. His dad worked in that building. He had been there when the attack happened. The enormity of it all weighed down on him, suffocating him with dread.

His mom tried to stay calm, but Alex could see the fear on her face. She kept the TV on, anxiously watching every update, hoping for good news, but none came. Every time a new report came in, her eyes would widen with fear, and she would quickly glance at Alex, trying to mask her worry. But Alex saw it. He felt it, too.

"It's going to be okay, Alex," she said, her voice soft but strained. "We'll hear something soon."

Alex wasn't so sure. The images of burning towers and ash-covered streets on the screen told a different story. His heart ached with the terrifying reality that his father might not come home. The hope that had flickered in his chest began to dim as the hours passed. Still, he couldn't stop hoping. He couldn't stop holding onto the small chance that his dad had somehow made it out.

Time seemed to stretch endlessly as they waited, each moment heavy with silence and dread. The phone didn't ring. No updates came. Alex sat on the couch next to his mom, his fingers gripping the edge of the cushion so tightly that his knuckles turned white. Every time the news anchors spoke, Alex's breath caught in his throat, but it was always the same—more reports of devastation, more stories of people lost, and no word about his father.

By night's fall, Alex's hope had shrunk to almost nothing. His mom's eyes were red from crying, and though she tried to be strong for him, Alex knew she was just as scared as he was. The world felt darker and heavier, like it had shifted in a way that could never be undone.

Alex lay in bed that night, staring up at the ceiling, his mind racing with images of the attack. He tried to hold onto the hope that his father might walk through the door, call, and somehow had survived. But as the night dragged on, his hope slipped further away, replaced by a hollow, aching fear.

September 13th, 2001

For two days, Alex had lived in limbo, clinging to the faintest shred of hope that somehow, against all odds, his father might have survived the collapse of the Twin Towers. Deep down, he knew the chances were slim, but until now, he had refused to believe the worst. But as the hours stretched into days, and the silence from his father became deafening, that hope shriveled into nothing.

Today, the confirmation came. His father was dead. Alex sat on the edge of his bed, staring blankly at the floor, unable to process the magnitude of the loss. His hands hung limply by his sides, his entire body feeling as though it was weighed down by something too heavy to carry. Everything felt surreal, like he was caught in a nightmare he couldn't wake up from. How could it be true? How could his dad—his strong, invincible dad be gone just like that?

The room around him was quiet, but his mind buzzed with an angry, frustrated confusion. How could someone do something like this? How could anyone have caused so much pain, so much devastation, and taken his dad away? The questions spun in his head, each cutting deeper, but there were no answers. Only the aching silence of loss.

His mom had told him earlier in the day. Her voice had been soft, trembling as she knelt beside him and whispered the words Alex had dreaded. He hadn't cried when she told him—he couldn't. The reality of it all was too big, too overwhelming to grasp fully. Instead, he nodded, his body numb, and retreated to his room.

Now, he sat alone, struggling to come to terms with a world where his dad no longer existed. It felt impossible. The man who had taught him how to ride a bike, stood beside him during those Thanksgiving dinners, and promised to be there after getting out of rehab—was gone. And Alex didn't know how to handle it. He felt like he was floating outside of himself, disconnected from everything.

The next few days went by in a blur. His mom planned, and family members came by to offer condolences, but Alex barely registered any of it. It all felt distant, like he was watching his life happen from behind a foggy window. People told him they were sorry and that his dad had been a hero, but none of it made the ache in his chest any lighter.

At night, Alex would lie in bed, staring at the ceiling, waiting for tears that wouldn't come. He missed his dad more than anything—more than he had ever thought possible. But somehow, he felt like he had cried all his tears in those first few hours after the news came. Now, all that was left was a deep, hollow emptiness. It scared him, how numb he felt. Shouldn't he be crying more? Shouldn't he be feeling more? But the emotions were trapped inside him, too tangled or heavy to bear.

The world around him continued to move, and people went about their lives, but for Alex, everything had stopped. He wasn't sure if things would ever feel normal again. His dad was gone, and with him, a part of Alex felt lost, too.

November 22nd, 2001

Thanksgiving had always been a day of family, food, and tradition for Alex. But this year, it was nothing like the ones he remembered. The house, usually warm with the smell of roasting turkey and his parents' chatter, now felt cold and empty. The only sound was the faint hum of the TV in the background and the soft, steady snoring of his mother passed out on the couch.

It had been two months since his father was killed in the 9/11 attacks, but the grief that weighed down on Alex's heart felt as raw as it had the day he found out. His mother had retreated into a world of her own since then, drowning her pain in alcohol, leaving Alex to fend for himself.

Thanksgiving, once his favorite holiday, now felt like another day, another reminder that everything had changed.

There was no food on the table, no turkey, no mashed potatoes, no pie. The fridge was nearly empty, and Alex's stomach growled painfully, but he had already gotten used to going to bed hungry. He had hoped that maybe, just for today, things would be different. Maybe his mom would wake up, perhaps they'd pull something together, maybe...just maybe, they'd find a way to have Thanksgiving like they used to. But as he looked at her slumped figure on the couch, a half-empty bottle of liquor lying beside her, that hope slowly faded.

The sight of his mother like this numb, absent, and unreachable was becoming more and more familiar. Since his father's death, the vibrant woman who used to make holidays special had disappeared, leaving behind someone who could barely function, someone who wasn't there anymore.

Alex sighed and glanced out the window, where he could see other families coming and going, likely heading to or from Thanksgiving dinners filled with laughter, warmth, and food. He imagined the tables piled high with turkey and sides, imagined the sound of clinking plates, and shared stories. But for him, those were just memories, distant and unreachable.

He sat on the floor beside the couch, his knees pulled up to his chest, and stared blankly at the TV. The holiday shows on the screen felt foreign, as if they belonged to another world. The warmth and cheer they portrayed felt like a cruel joke. All Alex could think about was how alone he felt, how much he missed his dad, and how much he wished for just one more Thanksgiving when they were together as a family.

But those days were gone, and Alex wondered if this was how it would always be now. His mom was drunk all the time, disappearing into her grief, leaving Alex to navigate the wreckage of their lives on his own. He was only ten years old, but he felt much older, weighed down by the kind of sadness and loneliness that no child should ever have to bear.

As the sun set outside, casting long shadows across the room, Alex realized he would be going to bed hungry again. The emptiness in his stomach mirrored the emptiness in the house, and with a heavy heart, he quietly got up and made his way to his room.

Lying in bed, Alex stared at the ceiling, the silence pressing around him. He couldn't help but wonder if this was his new way of life—no more holidays, warmth, or family. Just him, alone, trying to hold on to memories that seemed to slip further away with each passing day.

For the first time in his life, Alex wasn't sure if things would ever get better.

December 25th, 2001

Alex had hoped that this Christmas might be different. He had gone to bed the night before with a flicker of hope, thinking that maybe, just maybe, his mom would pull herself together for today. Perhaps she would get up early and sit together by the tree, sharing at least a moment of normalcy. But as he walked into the living room that Christmas morning, the familiar disappointment hit him like a weight on his chest.

His mother was passed out on the couch, drunk and half-naked, her body sprawled out carelessly, one arm dangling over the edge. Empty bottles littered the coffee table, and the TV was still on from the night before, casting a dull glow over the room. Alex's heart sank. He had seen this so many times now that it almost didn't surprise him anymore—but today, it hurt more than usual. Today was supposed to be special. It was Christmas, and he had hoped for something different, something better.

He stood there momentarily, watching her, a lump forming in his throat. He had thought about waking her up, had even reached out to shake her shoulder gently, but she was too far gone, lost in the haze of alcohol. She barely stirred, muttering something incoherent before sinking deeper into the cushions.

Alex let out a long, heavy sigh. This wasn't how he wanted to spend Christmas morning, but there was nothing he could do. His mom was unreachable, trapped in her grief, her pain. And once again, Alex was left to face the day alone.

He turned away from the couch, heading toward the kitchen. The house felt cold; the emptiness settled deep in the bones, making everything seem heavier. He rummaged through the fridge, searching for something to eat, but it was almost bare. There were no Christmas treats, no special breakfast waiting for him, just the usual leftovers and scraps. He grabbed a slice of bread, not even bothering to toast it, and sat at the kitchen table, chewing quietly, the silence pressing in around him.

Outside, the world seemed to carry on with its holiday cheer. He could hear the faint sounds of laughter from the neighbors, the distant hum of cars passing by, people going about their day, celebrating with family. But for Alex, Christmas was just another day, another day spent alone in a house that no longer felt like home.

As he stared at the half-eaten piece of bread, that lump in his throat grew tighter. He didn't want to cry, didn't want to let the sadness consume him, but it was hard not to. The weight of everything, the loss of his dad, the emptiness of the house, and his mother's growing absence were too much for a ten-year-old to carry. He wanted to be strong, but he felt...alone right now.

He thought about the Christmases they used to have when his dad was alive, and his mom was still herself. The tree would be lit with colorful lights and presents piled underneath, and the smell of cinnamon rolls would fill the house. They would sit together, laugh, and open gifts; for that day, everything felt perfect.

But those days were gone. The tree stood half-decorated in the corner, the lights dim and tangled, and there were no presents beneath it. His mom was a ghost of the woman she used to be, and the house was filled with a quiet sadness that seemed impossible to escape.

After finishing his meager breakfast, Alex went back to the living room. His mom hadn't moved. She lay there, her breathing shallowly, her face flushed from the alcohol. Alex looked at her, feeling a mixture of sadness and anger. He wanted to shake her, scream at her, wake up, and be his mom again, but he knew it wouldn't do any good.

Instead, he gently pulled a blanket from the armchair and draped it over her, covering her exposed skin. For a moment, he stood there, watching her, the lump in his throat making it hard to breathe.

With a sigh, Alex turned and walked back to his room. He knew this was how it would be, at least for now. He would spend Christmas alone, just like Thanksgiving, like so many days before. But even though he was used to it, it didn't hurt any less.

As he lay on his bed, staring at the ceiling, Alex closed his eyes and wished for something better. He hoped for the mom he used to know, for the dad who used to make Christmas memorable, for a life that didn't feel so broken.

But deep down, he knew that those wishes wouldn't come true. Not this year. Not for a long time.

January 1st, 2002

By now, Alex had grown accustomed to the sound of his mom stumbling through the front door late at night, the clink of empty bottles, and the acrid smell of cigarettes clinging to her clothes. It had become part of his life since his father died—his mom going out every weekend, drinking herself into a stupor, and returning home with strange men. It was like she had become a different person, slipping further and further away from the mother he once knew. And yet, despite everything, Alex still loved her.

New Year's morning was no different.

The house was eerily quiet, except for the muffled sound of snoring coming from his mother's bedroom. Alex lay in bed for a long time, staring at the ceiling, dreading what he already knew he would find when he got up. He had just hoped the new year might bring change and peace. But that hope had been fleeting, replaced by the familiar weight of disappointment.

When he finally dragged himself out of bed, he hesitated in the hallway, standing just outside his mom's bedroom door. The door was slightly ajar, and Alex could see the outline of his mom, who passed out in bed through the crack. But she wasn't alone. A man he didn't recognize lay beside her, his arm draped across her as they slept off the night before. The room reeked of alcohol and smoke, and the sight of it made Alex's stomach churn.

Anger welled up inside him, sharp and hot. How could she do this? How could she lie there with some stranger, like his father had never existed? It felt like a betrayal, not just to him but to the memory of his dad. His dad had only been gone for a few months, and already his mom had let herself spiral so far out of control, letting random men into their home, their lives. Alex's heart ached with the weight of it, all the grief, the anger, the confusion that he didn't know how to handle.

He turned away from the door, silently retreating to his room, his hands trembling with emotion. Once inside, he shut the door quietly behind him and sat down on his bed, his chest tight with a mix of sorrow and rage. He wanted to scream, to yell at his mom, to tell her how much it hurt to see her like this, to feel like she had abandoned him. But the words stuck in his throat, trapped beneath the crushing weight of his feelings.

Instead, the tears came. Alex buried his face in his hands, his body shaking as the sobs wracked through him. It wasn't fair. None of this was fair. He had lost his father most horrifically, and now he felt like he was losing his mother, too. Even though she was still there, physically, she wasn't the same. She wasn't the mom who used to laugh and bake cookies with him, who used to make Christmas special. She was someone else now—someone distant, someone broken.

Alex felt the anger and sadness blend as the tears fell, twisting into a knot of emotions he couldn't untangle. He loved his mom, but he hated what she had become. He hated the way she drowned her pain in alcohol, the way she let strangers into their home, the way she seemed to have forgotten everything they had once been as a family. Most of all, he hated how helpless he felt. There was nothing he could do to bring her back, nothing he could say to make her stop.

Eventually, the tears subsided, but the ache in his chest remained. Alex wiped his eyes with his shirt sleeve, staring at the floor, lost in thought. He wondered if this was how things would be from now on—if this was his life now—a life filled with empty bottles, strange men, and a mother who wasn't there anymore.

For the first time, Alex felt truly alone.

July 12th, 2002

Alex had learned to brace himself whenever his mom was around people. Since his dad died, her drinking had spiraled out of control, and she had embarrassed him more times than he could count. But on his 12th birthday, she managed to outdo even her worst moments.

The day had started with a glimmer of hope. Alex had thought maybe, just maybe, she could hold it together for his birthday. His aunt and her family were coming over, and he had hoped for a simple, quiet day—nothing extravagant, just something that resembled the birthdays he used to have before everything fell apart. But as soon as the doorbell rang and his aunt's family arrived, Alex could tell something was off.

His mom was already drunk.

She stumbled into the living room, her eyes glassy and unfocused, holding a drink that sloshed over the rim as she waved them inside. The smell of alcohol clung to her like a cloud, and Alex's stomach twisted with embarrassment. His aunt shot him a sympathetic look as they exchanged greetings, but the tension in the room was palpable. Alex tried to ignore it, hoping that things wouldn't get worse. But he knew better.

It didn't take long for the scene to spiral out of control. As they sat down to eat, his mom's behavior became more erratic.

She slurred her words, making loud, inappropriate jokes that no one laughed at. Then she started cursing at random, her voice rising as she grew more agitated for no reason Alex could understand. She knocked over a glass of wine, the red liquid pooling on the tablecloth, but instead of apologizing, she laughed and cursed at the mess. Everyone else sat in stunned silence, unsure of what to do.

Alex felt his face burn with humiliation, his heart pounding. He couldn't look at his aunt or his cousins. All he could think about was how much he wished he could disappear and how much he wanted this not to happen, especially today, on his birthday.

As his mom continued shouting, Alex's aunt tried to calm her down, gently suggesting that maybe it was time to take a break. But his mom only got angrier, throwing her hands up and swaying on her feet as she cursed at her sister. "I don't need anyone telling me what to do in my own house!" she yelled, her voice slurring.

Alex wanted to crawl into a hole and hide. This wasn't how it was supposed to be. Birthdays were supposed to be filled with laughter, presents, and cake—not drunken shouting and embarrassment. He could feel the stares of his cousins, awkward and uncomfortable, and it only made the knot of shame in his chest tighten.

Finally, his mom stumbled over to the couch, mumbling incoherently, and collapsed into the cushions. Within minutes, she was passed out, leaving the room in an uneasy silence. Alex stood there, frozen, his hands clenched into fists as the weight of everything pressed down on him.

His aunt quietly gathered her things, motioning for her family to follow. She gave Alex one more sympathetic glance as she hugged him goodbye. "I'm so sorry, Alex," she whispered, her voice heavy with pity. But that was the last thing Alex wanted pity.

As soon as they left, the house felt even emptier. The birthday decorations hung limply on the walls, and the cake sat untouched on the table. Alex stood alone in the middle of the room, staring at the mess his mother had made: the spilled wine, the overturned plates, and her slumped figure on the couch.

The tears threatened to come, but Alex held them back, swallowing hard as the lump in his throat grew. He had learned to live with disappointment and embarrassment, but today... today hurt more than usual. It wasn't just that his mom had embarrassed him in front of his family it was the realization that this was his life now. This was how it would always be.

Like so many other days, his birthday had been stolen from him, not by the death of his father this time, but by his mother's self-destruction.

Alex sat at the table, staring at the empty chair where his dad should have been. The silence in the house was deafening, and as much as he wanted to cry, he couldn't. All he felt was a hollow ache, the weight of everything settling deeper into his chest.

September 11th, 2002

It had been exactly one year since the day Alex's father died, and the weight of that anniversary hung heavy in the air. Alex had felt it all day at school—the ache of knowing that nothing would ever be the same, the sharp memories of what he'd lost. The whispers in the halls, the news coverage playing in classrooms, and the teacher's sympathetic looks only deepened the sadness he carried with him.

When he walked through the front door after school, Alex was hit with an overwhelming smell of alcohol. His heart sank. He knew what he would find before he even entered the living room. Sure enough, there was his mother, passed out on the couch, an empty bottle of bourbon lying beside her, her arm draped limply over the edge of the cushions. The TV blared in the background, but she didn't stir.

The sight had become painfully familiar over the past year. His mother had always struggled with alcohol after his dad's death, but today, on the first anniversary, it seemed worse. The house felt suffocating, the smell of stale liquor clinging to everything. Alex stood in the doorway, his backpack still hanging from one shoulder, and for a moment, he just stared at her, feeling an all-too-familiar mix of sadness, frustration, and helplessness.

He knew he had to stay strong for her—he had been telling himself that for months. He had taken on more responsibility than any twelve-year-old should have to, cleaning up after her, making sure she got to bed when she drank too much, and doing his best to hold things together when she couldn't. But it was getting harder and harder to do that. Every day felt like a battle; no matter how much he tried, it was never enough.

Today, it hurt more than usual. Today, the empty place where his father should have been felt like a gaping wound that would never heal.

Alex dropped his backpack on the floor and walked over to the couch, kneeling beside his mom. Her face was pale, her hair a tangled mess, and the lines of grief etched into her features seemed more profound than ever. He gently shook her shoulder, but she didn't wake up. She muttered something under her breath, but it was incoherent, lost in the haze of alcohol.

Alex sighed, the heaviness in his chest threatening to pull him under. He couldn't do this much longer. He couldn't keep pretending everything would be okay when it wasn't. His mother was slipping further away from him, and no matter how much he tried to stay strong, he couldn't fix her. He couldn't bring his dad back. And today, of all days, that realization hit him harder than ever.

Sitting back on his heels, Alex wiped a tear from his cheek before it could fall. He wished his dad was still around. He wished he didn't have to be the one to carry all of this weight alone. His mom needed help, and so did he. But help wasn't coming. His father wasn't coming back. It was just him and his mom, and that truth hurt more than anything.

He stood up and grabbed the empty bourbon bottle, setting it aside with the others. Then he pulled a blanket from the armchair and gently draped it over his mother, covering her as best as possible. She wouldn't wake up for hours; by then, she would be groggy and distant, barely acknowledging him. It was the same routine, repeatedly, and Alex was exhausted from it.

As he walked back to his room, the house felt too quiet, too empty, and the echo of what used to be a family was now reduced to the silence of loss. Alex sat down on his bed, his eyes staring blankly at the wall, wondering how long he could keep pretending he was strong enough to hold everything together.

For the first time in a long while, Alex let himself cry. The tears came slowly at first, but then they poured out, releasing all the fear, frustration, and sorrow he had held in for so long. He missed his dad more than he could ever put into words. And today, on the anniversary of his death, that pain felt sharper than ever.

He wiped his eyes, took a deep breath, and tried to compose himself. But even as the tears dried, the ache remained, a constant reminder that things would never be the same.

October 2nd, 2002

It had been over a year since Alex's life had been turned upside down, and in that time, he had grown used to being alone. The other kids at school didn't beat him up anymore, not since his father died in the 9/11 attacks, but the loneliness hadn't gone away. Most of his so-called 'friends' were just classmates who pitied him. They were kind enough, but Alex could feel the distance between them as if they were always holding back. He had spent so much time feeling like an outsider he had almost forgotten what it was like to connect with someone.

That all changed when Mark moved into the house down the street.

Alex had been riding his bike one Saturday afternoon when he noticed the moving truck parked in front of the old, empty house on the corner. Curious, he rode over and saw a boy about his age standing outside, watching as boxes and furniture were carried into the house. The boy looked over, their eyes met, and before Alex knew it, they were talking.

Mark had an easy way about him, a friendly smile that made Alex feel comfortable immediately. They talked about simple things at first—school, video games, sports. But soon, they were running around the neighborhood together, playing catch in the yard, racing their bikes down the street. It all happened so quickly that Alex almost couldn't believe it.

For the first time in what felt like forever, Alex didn't feel like he had to be anyone but himself.

There was something different about Mark. He didn't know about Alex's past, bullying, the loss, or the pity that usually followed Alex wherever he went. He didn't see Alex as the kid whose father had died in the towers. To Mark, Alex was just a kid, just another friend. And that felt like a breath of fresh air.

The two boys played together, climbed trees, rode bikes, and played video games at Mark's new house. There was an ease in their friendship that Alex had never felt before. He didn't have to put on a brave face or pretend that everything was fine or that he was someone he wasn't. With Mark, he could just be himself without fear of judgment or pity. It was the first time in a long while that Alex felt... normal.

Alex sometimes felt like an outsider at school, but with Mark he never did. They laughed at the same dumb jokes, raced each other on their bikes until they were out of breath, and talked about everything and nothing. For the first time since his dad died, Alex didn't feel like he was carrying the weight of the world on his shoulders.

He was amazed at how easy it was to talk to Mark. The conversations flowed naturally, and there was no need to hide or pretend. It wasn't like the forced, awkward conversations he sometimes had with kids at school who only talked to him out of sympathy. This was real. For the first time, Alex didn't feel like he had to prove anything to anyone.

As the sun set that evening and the two boys sat on the curb, tossing rocks into the street and laughing about something ridiculous, Alex realized something important. This was what friendship was supposed to feel like easy, natural, and real. And for the first time in a long while, he felt like he wasn't alone.

October 15th, 2002

Alex knew something was wrong when Mark stopped coming to his house after school. At first, it was subtle—Mark's parents were making excuses, saying he couldn't come over that day because they had plans or were too busy. But it didn't take long for the truth to come out. One day, Mark told Alex the real reason. His parents didn't want him at Alex's house anymore. They said it was because of his mom.

Alex wasn't surprised. His mom had been drinking more and more since his dad's death, and it had become impossible to ignore. She was constantly stumbling around the house, slurring her words, and sometimes appearing unannounced at Mark's house, embarrassing him and Alex. Alex knew it wasn't fair to Mark. He knew what it was like to feel embarrassed by her, but hearing it from someone else stung him in a way that was hard to describe.

Mark's parents didn't want their son around "that kind of influence." That's how they had put it—like Alex's house was toxic, like his mother's drinking was something dangerous that could infect their son. Alex had always tried to ignore the shame that came with his mom's behavior, but hearing it said out loud, knowing that people saw his home that way, made it so much worse.

Mark still wanted to be friends. That was the one silver lining in all of this. Despite his parents ' objections, Mark wasn't ready to give up on their friendship. So, they adapted. Instead of playing at Alex's house, they met outside after school, racing their bikes to the park or playing in the street until Mark went home for dinner. It wasn't the same, but it was something. It was a way to hold onto the one good thing in Alex's life.

But the hurt lingered no matter how hard Alex tried to push it aside. He hated that his mom's drinking had ruined yet another part of his life, and every time he walked home alone after spending time with Mark, the weight of it all pressed down on him. His mom was never going to change—she was too lost in her grief, too far gone into the world of alcohol. And now, because of that, he couldn't even have his best friend over to his house.

There was a kind of quiet shame in knowing that his home, where he was supposed to feel safe, was seen as something to avoid. It wasn't just the embarrassment—it was the reminder that his family wasn't typical, that his mom wasn't like other moms. She was broken, and no matter how much Alex wished for things to get better, he knew they wouldn't.

But as the days passed, Alex clung to his friendship with Mark. Playing in the park, shooting hoops, and racing down the street became the highlights of his day. Even though they couldn't hang out at his house, Mark never treated Alex differently. He didn't pity or treat him like he was broken, and Alex was grateful.

Still, every time Alex saw Mark heading back to his house where dinner would be waiting, where his parents were present and sober, his chest ache grew slightly heavier. It wasn't jealousy, exactly. It was more like a longing, a reminder of everything he had lost, everything that had been taken from him when his dad died.

And as much as Alex cherished his friendship with Mark, there was always that nagging thought: how long would it last before Mark's parents took him away?

October 31st, 2002

Halloween had started as one of Alex's best nights in a long time. He and Mark spent the evening running from house to house, their plastic pumpkins heavy with candy as they laughed and joked their way through the neighborhood. The cool autumn air felt crisp; the streets were alive with kids in costumes, porch lights glowing, and the occasional spooky decoration that made them laugh even harder. Alex forgot everything else for a few hours, such as his mom and daily responsibilities, and just enjoyed being a kid.

When they returned to Alex's house, their bags were full of candy, and Alex felt lighter than he had in months. But his heart sank as they turned the corner, and his house appeared.

His mother was standing in the front yard. She was yelling at a group of kids from the neighborhood, her voice slurred and angry. Alex could see it from a distance—the way she swayed unsteadily, waving her arms in the air, her face flushed from drinking. The kids looked confused, some laughing nervously while others just hurried away.

Alex's stomach tightened with embarrassment. He could feel the shame creeping up his spine, making his face burn. This was the last thing he wanted Mark to see. He had tried hard to keep his home life separate from his friendship with Mark, but now it was fully displayed. His mother was drunk again and making a scene in front of everyone.

Mark noticed, too, and the lightness of the night faded. He tried to make a joke, to brush it off, but Alex couldn't even force a smile. All he wanted to do was disappear, to go inside and hide from the world. He didn't want Mark to see his mom like this. He didn't want anyone to see her like this.

As they approached the house, Alex's mom turned her attention to him and Mark. Her eyes were glassy, and she wobbled as she tried to focus on them. "Alex! There you are!" she called out, her words slurring together. "Look at all the candy you got! Ha! Bet you didn't need any help with that, did you?"

Her voice was too loud, her laughter too forced, and Alex cringed. He could feel Mark's eyes on him but couldn't bring himself to meet his friend's gaze. The shame was too heavy, pressing down on him like a weight he couldn't escape.

"Mom, let's go inside," Alex muttered, his voice barely above a whisper. He didn't want to make a scene. He just wanted this to end.

His mom wasn't done. She continued shouting at the other kids as they walked by, throwing curses and slurred insults that made Alex's skin crawl. The neighbors were watching now, whispering to one another, and Alex felt like he was shrinking, like the whole world was closing in on him.

Mark, sensing Alex's discomfort, put a hand on his shoulder. "It's okay, man," he said softly. "Let's just go inside."

But for Alex, the damage was done. He wanted nothing more than to hide to escape the embarrassment and the anger building inside him. His mom had done this before, but somehow, having Mark there made it worse. It wasn't just the shame of her drunken antics. It was the fear that Mark would see him differently now, that this moment would change everything.

They eventually made it inside, and Alex locked the door behind them, shutting out the chaos from the front yard. But the night had already been ruined. The joy of trick-or-treating, laughter, and fun was all gone, replaced by the heavy weight of his mother's behavior.

Alex sat at the kitchen table, staring at the pile of candy he and Mark had worked so hard to collect. But now, it didn't seem to matter. All he could think about was the embarrassment, the sinking feeling in his chest, and the overwhelming sense of helplessness that came with being the child of a mother who was spiraling further out of control.

Mark sat beside him, quietly sorting through his candy, acting like nothing had happened. But Alex couldn't shake the feeling that things had changed. It had been a long night, made even longer by the weight of his mother's actions.

November 28th, 2002

Alex had never felt so grateful for an invitation in his life. Mark's family had asked him to spend Thanksgiving with them, and Alex had jumped at the chance. He couldn't stand the thought of spending another holiday at home, surrounded by the silence and the smell of alcohol. His mother had been passed out drunk since the early afternoon, and the house felt more like a tomb than a home. Thanksgiving, once a day filled with warmth and family, had become just another reminder of everything he had lost.

When Alex arrived at Mark's house, the difference was immediate. The warmth hit him as soon as he walked in—both from the kitchen's heat and the cheerful atmosphere that filled the house. The smell of roasted turkey, mashed potatoes, and pies baking in the oven was almost overwhelming. Mark's parents were laughing and joking, their voices mingling with the clatter of dishes and the hum of holiday music in the background. It was everything Alex had once had and everything he missed.

As much as he appreciated the kindness of Mark's family, a deep sadness settled over him as the evening went on. He couldn't shake the thoughts of his mother, who passed out on the couch at home, her life spiraling further out of control with each passing day. She used to be the one who made Thanksgiving special, who filled their house with the smells of homemade stuffing and pies, and who laughed as she called everyone to the table. Now, that version of her was replaced by someone who could barely hold herself together.

Sitting at the table with Mark's family, Alex felt like an outsider. Everyone was trying so hard to make him feel welcome, to act like nothing was wrong, but Alex could feel the weight of their pity. He saw the glances they exchanged when they thought he wasn't looking—the sad, knowing looks that told him they felt sorry for him and, worse, their thinly veiled disgust for his mother.

He knew they were trying to be kind, but it only made him feel more out of place. The laughter and the jokes all felt hollow to him, as if he were watching a scene from a movie that he wasn't a part of. He could feel their pity seeping into every interaction, and it gnawed at him, reminding him of how different his life was now. They pitied him for what he had to deal with at home, for what his mother had become, and that pity only made the ache in his chest grow deeper.

As Mark's parents passed around the turkey and everyone started digging in, Alex forced himself to smile and pretend he was okay. He didn't want to ruin the evening. He didn't want Mark or his family to feel awkward because of him. But inside, the sadness felt like a weight pressing down on him. It wasn't just about missing his dad—it was about missing the version of his mother who had once made holidays feel special—the version of her who was sober, who cared, who was present.

Now, she was just...gone. Not physically, but in every other way that mattered.

Sensing that something was off, Mark leaned over and whispered, "Hey, are you okay?" His voice was soft and full of concern.

Alex nodded, swallowing hard. "Yeah, I'm fine," he lied. But the truth was, he wasn't fine, he hadn't been fine in a long time.

The rest of the evening passed in a blur. Alex tried to focus on the food and conversation, but his mind drifted back to his mother. The image of her lying on the couch, oblivious to the world, haunted him. He hated what she had become and even more that he couldn't do anything to fix it. No matter how hard he tried to hold things together, it was never enough.

As dessert was served, Alex excused himself to the bathroom, needing to be alone. He stared at his reflection in the mirror, his eyes tired and hollow. The laughter and warmth from the dining room felt a world away. He wiped his face with his hands, trying to shake off the sadness, but it clung to him like a shadow.

When he returned to the table, Mark's parents were still chatting and laughing, acting like everything was normal. And maybe for them, it was. But for Alex, nothing felt normal anymore.

December 25th, 2002

Christmas was supposed to be a time of joy and celebration, but for Alex, it had become a day filled with dread. His mother had been drinking heavily for the past year, but this time, it was different. They were at Mark's family's house for Christmas dinner, and she had been drinking since the morning. At first, Alex had hoped she might keep it together, but as the evening wore on, it became clear that wouldn't happen.

His mother had started making crude jokes at the dinner table, loud and inappropriate comments that left the entire room in awkward silence. Mark's parents exchanged uncomfortable glances; their smiles strained as they tried to maintain some sense of normalcy. But Alex could see it how their eyes flickered with frustration and embarrassment. They didn't know what to do, and neither did Alex. All he could feel was the slow, creeping humiliation as his mom continued to act ridiculous, oblivious to the effect she was having on everyone around her.

She was slurring her words, laughing too loudly at her jokes, her face flushed from the alcohol. Alex winced every time she opened her mouth, knowing that more embarrassment was on the way. He had seen her drunk before too many times but never like this, never in front of other people, and certainly not in front of Mark's family, who had been nothing but kind to him.

Alex wanted to disappear, to crawl under the table and hide from the shame that was building inside him. He wished more than anything that she would stop and realize what she was doing, but it was like she was completely unaware of how her behavior was affecting everyone in the room.

The tension around the table was unbearable. Mark's parents were trying to remain polite, but Alex could see the tightness in their smiles, the way they glanced at each other when his mom wasn't looking. Mark sat quietly beside him, his eyes downcast, clearly uncomfortable, and not wanting to make things worse. The festive cheer that had filled the room earlier had vanished, replaced by a thick, awkward silence that seemed to grow with every passing minute.

Finally, Alex couldn't take it anymore. His heart pounded as he stood up from the table, swallowing his pride. He grabbed his mother by the arm gently but firmly. "Mom, we need to go," he whispered, trying to keep his voice calm, even though inside, he felt like screaming. She resisted at first, laughing it off, but Alex was done. He couldn't stand another minute of watching her embarrass herself—and him—in front of people who didn't deserve to deal with this.

"Come on, let's go," he said, louder this time, pulling her to her feet.

His mother protested, her voice slurring, but Alex didn't care. He kept his grip on her arm and steered her toward the door.

As they moved, he glanced back at Mark's parents, his face flushed with embarrassment. "I'm sorry," he mumbled, his throat tight with shame. "I'm so sorry about all of this."

Mark's parents nodded, their expressions softening with sympathy. They could see how hard this was for Alex, but the pity in their eyes only made it worse. He hated that they had to see this side of his life and witness how broken everything had become.

Outside, the cold air hit them like a shock, and Alex's mom stumbled, nearly losing her balance. He tightened his grip, guiding her down the steps, feeling the weight of the evening settle over him. His heart ached with frustration, anger, and sadness all mixed in a way that left him feeling hollow.

As they walked away from the house, his mom mumbled something incoherent, unaware of the damage she had done. But Alex didn't respond. He was too tired—tired of cleaning up after her, tired of apologizing for her, and tired of the constant embarrassment that came with being her son.

Christmas, once a day of magic and warmth, had become something he dreaded. And as he led his mother home, the weight of that reality pressed down on him harder than ever.

July 12th, 2003

Alex had been looking forward to his 13th birthday for months. It felt like a milestone—finally becoming a teenager. He was excited to celebrate the day with his best friend, Mark, and Mark's family. For once, he hoped things would go smoothly. Maybe this year would be different. Maybe his mom would keep it together, and he could enjoy his birthday like a normal kid. But deep down, Alex knew better.

The party had started well enough. Mark and his family had come over, bringing a cake and presents, trying to make the day special. For a while, it seemed like it might work. His mom had kept to herself, sitting quietly in the corner of the living room, sipping her drink. But as the afternoon wore on, that uneasy feeling in Alex's chest grew. He could tell by the way his mother's laughter grew louder, by the way her eyes glazed over, that it wouldn't be long before things went south, and then, just as Alex was starting to relax, his worst fears came true.

It started with a small comment. One of Mark's parents said something innocent about how fast Alex was growing up, but it set his mom off for some reason. She slammed her drink down on the table, her face flushed from the alcohol, and stood up, her voice rising.

"Judgmental hypocrites!" she spat, her words slurring. "You all think you're better than me, right?"

The room fell silent. Everyone froze, unsure of what to say or do. Alex's heart sank as the tension thickened. He could feel all eyes on him, but he could do nothing to stop it. His mom was in one of her moods; when that happened, there was no turning back.

She continued, her voice growing louder, her accusations more wild. "You come into my house, pretend to be so nice, but I see how you look at me! You think I don't know? You think I'm some joke?" She stumbled as she gestured wildly, nearly knocking over a chair. "You're all just a bunch of judgmental hypocrites!"

Alex could feel his face burning with embarrassment. His stomach twisted into knots, and he wished more than anything that he could disappear and somehow rewind time and erase this entire day. This was supposed to be his birthday, but his mom was ruining it, turning it into another one of her drunken disasters.

Mark sat awkwardly next to him, his face tense with discomfort. His parents stood, glancing at each other with wide eyes, unsure how to handle the situation. Alex could see the pity in their faces, but it only made him feel worse. This wasn't how it was supposed to be. This wasn't how any of it was supposed to be.

Finally, his mom collapsed onto the couch, her rant losing steam as she muttered more insults. The room was filled with an unbearable silence, the tension hanging thick in the air. Alex felt like the walls were closing in on him, the weight of humiliation pressing down harder with every passing second.

"I'm... I'm sorry," Alex mumbled, barely able to meet Mark's parents' eyes. He could feel the tears threatening to spill, but he forced them back. "I'm sorry."

Mark's family quickly gathered their things, murmuring awkward goodbyes as they hurried out the door. Alex stood in the living room, watching them leave, the shame curling tightly in his chest. He had never felt so humiliated in his life. His birthday, the day he had hoped might be different, had turned into a disaster. His mother, once again, had ruined everything.

As the door closed behind them, Alex looked over at his mom, who was now half-asleep on the couch, oblivious to the damage she had done. The anger and sadness bubbled up inside him, but there was nowhere for it to go. He was used to this by now, but that didn't make it any easier.

From then on, Alex promised himself he wouldn't invite anyone again. He couldn't take the embarrassment, couldn't handle the constant disappointment. It was easier to keep people at a distance, to hide his life from the world, rather than risk another day like this.

His 13th birthday was supposed to be a special day, but it had only served as a painful reminder of how far things had fallen apart.

September 11th, 2003

When Alex came home from school, the house was too quiet. He dropped his backpack by the door and called out for his mom, but there was no response. A familiar unease settled over him as he walked through the house, his footsteps echoing in the stillness. It had been two years since his father had died in the towers, but today felt different—heavier. He couldn't explain it, but something about the silence was suffocating.

When he reached the bathroom, he stopped in his tracks. The door was half open, the light spilling out into the hallway. At first, he didn't want to look. Something deep inside him told him not to, but he pushed the door open anyway.

The sight that greeted him was worse than anything he could have imagined.

His mother lay slumped in the bathtub, an empty vodka bottle resting between her legs. Blood smeared the tiles and splattered across the walls in horrific, jagged streaks. Alex's heart stopped when he saw the gun lying by her side and the unmistakable gunshot wound to her head. The world seemed to tilt, everything blurring as the realization hit him like a physical blow.

This couldn't be real. This couldn't be happening. A scream ripped through him, raw and desperate. He fell to his knees beside the tub, his hands trembling as he reached for her. Her skin was cold and stiff, and the emptiness in her eyes told him what he already knew. She was gone. There was nothing he could do. He screamed again, louder this time, hoping somehow that someone, anyone, would hear him and make this nightmare end. But it was too late. She was gone, and there was no coming back.

For hours, Alex sat there, his back pressed against the cold tile where the bathtub met the wall, holding his mother's icy hand as the minutes passed in agonizing silence. The tears came in waves, uncontrollable sobs that shook his entire body. He cried until his throat burned, until his chest ached, and he couldn't cry anymore. His world had ended once when his father died, and now it had shattered again. The final, brutal blow had been dealt.

As the hours dragged on, the light outside began to fade. Alex barely noticed. Time seemed meaningless in that moment, a blur of pain and disbelief. All he could do was sit there, gripping his mother's hand, as if somehow holding on would keep her close for a little longer.

Alex's mind raced, flashing through the memories of the arguments, the drunken nights, and the brief moments of clarity. He had known she was struggling, but he had never imagined this. He had never thought she would go this far. It felt like some sick, twisted joke that the anniversary of his father's death would end like this.

Eventually, the sobs quieted, replaced by a hollow, numb feeling that settled deep in his chest. The sun had gone down, casting long shadows through the window, and the house was quieter than before. Alex knew what he had to do next. He had to call the police and tell them what had happened. But the thought of it felt unbearable. It would make everything real, too real. There would be no going back.

With trembling hands, he finally let go of his mother's cold hand and stood up, his legs weak beneath him. He walked to the phone, each step heavy, his body numb with shock. When he picked up the receiver, his fingers shook as he dialed the number.

"911, what's your emergency?"

Alex's voice cracked as he spoke, barely a whisper. "My mom... she... she's gone."

September 28th, 2003

Alex moved through his room like a ghost, packing his bags in a daze. Every item he placed into the suitcase felt like another layer of his old life slipping away. He was leaving—he had to—but knowing that didn't make it any easier. The numbness he felt was all-consuming, a protective shield against the storm of emotions brewing beneath the surface. His mother was gone, and now, so was the life he had known.

His aunt had offered to take him in, but the thought of living in her cramped, unfamiliar house filled him with dread. It was small, smelled like mothballs, and nothing about it felt like home. But home wasn't an option anymore. The house he grew up in, where his parents had lived, was no longer a place he could stay. It was filled with too many memories and too much pain. It was a place of ghosts.

Alex zipped his suitcase closed, staring at the bare walls of his room, his heart heavy. The numbness started to crack, and a deep, simmering anger boiled underneath it. He felt it growing every time he thought about his mom and how she had left him, how she had made this decision without thinking about the destruction it would leave behind. The anger mixed with the grief, swirling together until it became a knot of pain so tight that Alex didn't know how to unravel it.

But more than anything, he was angry that he had to say goodbye to his best friend, Mark.

Alex had sworn, more times than he could count, that he and Mark would never be apart. They had been through so much together, and their friendship had been the one constant in Alex's life. But now, standing at the edge of his old life, Alex knew he couldn't stay. And as much as he tried to tell himself that they would keep in touch, that things wouldn't change, he couldn't ignore the sinking feeling that this goodbye was final.

The two boys stood outside, under the same tree they'd played under for years, neither knowing what to say. Mark kicked at the dirt, his hands stuffed into his pockets, while Alex stood staring at the ground with his suitcase on his feet. They had never imagined this day would come, and they never thought they would have to face the reality of saying goodbye.

"So... I guess this is it," Mark mumbled, his voice thick with emotion.

Alex nodded, his throat too tight to speak. He could feel the sting of tears behind his eyes, but he refused to let them fall. He had cried too much already—he couldn't do it again. Not now.

"I wish you didn't have to go," Mark added, his voice quieter.

"Me too," Alex finally whispered, his voice barely audible. "But I have to."

They knew it was true, but that didn't make it any easier. The weight of everything—the loss, the anger, the sadness settled over Alex like a suffocating blanket, making it hard to breathe. He wanted to say something else that would make this moment less painful, but the words wouldn't come. Instead, all he felt was the emptiness left behind by his mother's suicide, the hole that had ripped through his heart and left nothing but anger in its wake.

Finally, Mark looked up, his eyes glassy with unshed tears. "We'll still hang out, right? I mean, you'll visit?"

"Yeah," Alex said, but the word felt hollow. He didn't know what the future held. He didn't know if he'd ever be able to return to this place, to the life that had crumbled around him.

They hugged briefly, awkwardly, and then it was time. Alex grabbed his suitcase and walked away, leaving behind the only friend he had ever truly known. As he climbed into his aunt's car and they pulled away, the tears finally came, hot and stinging but silent. He didn't look back at Mark or the house that had once been his home. He couldn't.

At his aunt's house, the smell of mothballs hit him when he walked through the door, a sharp reminder of how different his life had become. The rooms were small and cramped, the furniture old and worn. Everything about it felt foreign, wrong. Alex stood in the doorway of his new room, the anger still bubbling beneath the surface, threatening to boil over.

He dropped his suitcase on the bed, staring at the unfamiliar surroundings. His heart ached with the loss of everything he had known, and the grief weighed down on him like a heavy stone. He tried not to think about his mom—about the gunshot, the blood, the emptiness she had left behind—but the images were burned into his mind.

As he sat on the edge of the bed, staring out the window, Alex wondered if this was his life now—cramped, lonely, filled with anger and a sense of betrayal that he couldn't shake. He didn't know if things would ever feel normal again. All he knew was that he had to keep going, even if it felt like his world had ended.

November 14th, 2003

Life at his aunt's house had never been easy for Alex. From the moment he arrived, it felt like he didn't belong. The cramped rooms, the lingering smell of mothballs, and the constant tension made it clear that this was not a home but a place to stay. But worse than the uncomfortable surroundings was how his aunt's family treated him. There was no kindness, no compassion. Instead, there was yelling, insults, and even the occasional slap when they felt he had done something wrong.

He didn't know why they were so cruel to him, why they couldn't see that he was already struggling, that he was still grieving the loss of both his parents. It seemed like he was just a burden to them—a reminder of something they didn't want to deal with. Every day was filled with harsh words and cold looks, and Alex had begun to wonder if he would ever feel loved or wanted again.

The breaking point came one evening after dinner. His aunt had snapped at him over something small; he hadn't cleaned the dishes fast enough, and before he knew it, she was shouting at him, calling him lazy and useless. Her words cut deep, each one like a knife twisting in his chest. Then came the slap, sharp and stinging, leaving Alex standing there, shocked and humiliated.

Something inside him broke as he lay in bed staring at the ceiling that night. He couldn't take it anymore. He couldn't live like this, constantly walking on eggshells, waiting for the next insult and slap. He had already lost so much—his father, his mother, his home. Now, it felt like he was losing himself, too, piece by piece. So, Alex decided., he was going to leave.

He waited until the house was quiet, until everyone else had gone to bed, and then he started packing. He didn't have much—just a few clothes, a picture of his parents, and a few small belongings he couldn't bear to leave behind. Everything fit into a small, worn-out backpack. His hands shook as he zipped it up, not with fear but with a strange mix of determination and desperation. He didn't know where he was going or what he would do, but he knew one thing for sure: he couldn't stay here any longer.

Quietly, he slipped out of bed and crept through the darkened house, careful not to make a sound. His heart pounded as he tiptoed down the hallway, past the door to his aunt's room. Every creak of the floorboards felt like a thunderclap in the silence, but no one stirred. Finally, he reached the front door, his hand resting on the cold doorknob for just a moment before he turned it and stepped outside.

The cool night air hit him like a wave, and Alex could breathe for the first time in what felt like forever. The sky above him was dark and dotted with stars, the world quiet and still. He stood there for a moment, taking it all in, before he began walking, his bag slung over his shoulder, his footsteps barely making a sound on the empty street.

He didn't have a plan. He didn't know where he would go or how long he could live alone, but none of that mattered. All he knew was that he needed to get away, to escape the place that had made him feel so unloved, so unwanted. He needed to find something—anything—that could give him a sense of peace, a sense of hope.

As he walked further from the house, the weight of everything began to lift. The anger, sadness, and feelings of worthlessness were still there, but now they were muted, softened by the freedom of leaving it all behind. Alex didn't know what lay ahead, but for the first time in a long time, he felt a spark of something he thought he had lost: control over his own life.

He didn't know where he was going, but he was free.

December 21st, 2003

Thirteen was too young to live on the streets, but Alex had no choice. He had been on his own for weeks, moving from place to place, trying to find shelter where he could. Some nights, he slept in doorways, bridges, or alleys. His clothes were dirty, his stomach constantly growling from hunger, and he had grown used to begging for food and spare change. He had learned how to survive, but nothing could have prepared him for what happened that night.

It was cold, the biting December wind cutting through his thin jacket as he huddled under an overpass, hoping to escape the chill. His breath came out in small puffs of mist, and he tried to pull his knees closer to his chest to stay warm. The streets were quieter than usual, the kind of quiet that always made Alex feel uneasy. He was always alert, watching, and aware of the dangers around him. But tonight, he was too tired, too worn out to move. He just wanted to sleep. Then he saw the man approach.

At first, Alex didn't think much of it. People walked by all the time, but something about how this man moved and his eyes locked onto Alex made his heart race with fear. He wanted to run, to get away, but his body wouldn't cooperate. The exhaustion, the cold, and hunger weighed him down and kept him frozen as the man got closer.

When the man was only a few feet away, Alex's instincts screamed at him to move, but it was too late. The man lunged, and the pain came suddenly, sharp and unbearable. The first punch knocked the wind out of Alex, sending him sprawling onto the cold, unforgiving concrete. He tried to scream, but nothing came out. His voice caught in his throat as the man's hands wrapped around his neck, choking him. The world spun as Alex gasped for air, his vision blurring as he struggled to breathe.

The man's weight pressed down on him, pinning him to the ground. Alex fought with everything he had, but the man was too strong. His fists slammed into Alex's body, each blow sending waves of agony through him. The concrete beneath him felt like ice, hard and unyielding, as the man punched him again, slamming Alex's head into the ground. A bright, blinding light flashed before Alex's eyes, and for a moment, he felt like he was floating—detached from the pain, from everything.

But then he felt the man's hands on his clothes, felt his pants being pulled off. Panic surged through Alex, but his body wouldn't respond. He couldn't move, couldn't scream, couldn't do anything but lie there as the man's weight bore down on him.

It was over in what felt like just a few minutes but stretched on for an eternity. Alex's mind went numb, retreating somewhere far away as his body endured the assault. When it was finally over, he heard the man's breath, heavy and labored, and felt his rough hands on his skin as he pulled away.

Then came the sharp, searing pain. Something pierced Alex's side, a cold, metallic feeling that sent a wave of fire through his body. He gasped, choking on his breath as he felt the blood begin to pour from the wound. The man stood up, pulling his pants back on, his face emotionless, as if what he had just done was routine.

Alex lay there, unable to move, his body trembling uncontrollably. He could feel his life slipping away with every drop of blood that soaked into the concrete. The coldness of the night crept deeper into his bones, but his mind was somewhere else, floating away as the world around him faded.

Before everything went black, Alex finally saw the man walking away, disappearing into the shadows as if he had never been there, and then, the darkness swallowed him whole.

December 27th, 2003

When Alex opened his eyes, the harsh, sterile light of the hospital room flooded his vision, and for a moment, he didn't know where he was. His body ached in ways he couldn't describe, a deep, unrelenting pain that throbbed with every heartbeat. He shifted slightly, feeling the tug of IV lines and the dull, persistent ache in his side. Then the memories crashed over him like a wave dark, suffocating, and too real to push away. He had been beaten, stabbed, and raped.

The details flashed through his mind, fragmented and terrifying, but he tried to push them away. He didn't want to remember, didn't want to relive the horror of what had happened to him under the overpass. But no matter how hard he tried, the image of the man, the feel of his hands, the sharp sting of the knife, they all clung to him, refusing to leave him in peace.

Alex stared at the ceiling, his chest tightening with fear and anger and something else he couldn't name. The hospital room was quiet except for the steady beep of the heart monitor and the occasional murmur of voices in the hallway. But inside his head, the noise was deafening. He had never felt so alone, so utterly abandoned by the world.

It had been hard living alone, much more challenging than he had ever imagined. When he first ran away, he thought he could survive, that anything would be better than staying with his aunt's family. But the streets had been unforgiving, cruel. Every day was a struggle, and every night was a new battle with hunger, cold, and fear. He thought he could handle it, but the reality was far harsher than anticipated.

As he lay there, his body broken and bruised, Alex couldn't help but think about all the other kids his age kids who were living everyday lives. They were probably getting ready for school, spending time with their families, playing video games, or hanging out with friends. They didn't have to worry about where their next meal would come from or whether they'd survive the night. They had homes, parents, and safety. And here he was, lying in a hospital bed after experiencing the worst kind of nightmare.

A bitter lump formed in his throat as he thought about what his life used to be before everything fell apart. He remembered going to school, hanging out with Mark, laughing, and feeling like the world was full of possibilities. Those days seemed so far away now, as if they belonged to someone else's life. He couldn't go back to those days. He couldn't go back to being the person he used to be.

Alex squeezed his eyes shut, trying to block out the flood of emotions that threatened to overwhelm him. Fear, shame, anger, and grief, all of it crashing into him at once. He wished, more than anything, that he wasn't alone. He wished he had someone to turn to, hold him, and tell him everything would be okay. But there was no one. Not anymore.

His parents were gone. Mark was far away, living a life Alex could no longer be a part of. And the streets... the streets had chewed him up and spit him out, leaving him broken and scarred.

The weight of it all pressed down on him, making breathing hard. He didn't know what to do, didn't know how to move forward. All he knew was that he couldn't stay here, trapped in this endless cycle of pain and fear. But he had no idea how to escape it or if he could.

As the minutes ticked by, Alex lay there in the quiet of the hospital room, his thoughts swirling in a dark, endless loop. He had survived, but what came next? How was he supposed to keep going when everything around him felt hopeless?

He didn't have the answers but could only close his eyes and wait for now. Wait for the pain to dull, the world to make sense again, and maybe find some way to survive.

January 14th, 2004

The day Alex was discharged from the hospital felt like the final blow. His body had mostly healed, but the emotional scars ran deep, and nothing felt real anymore. The social worker assigned to his case didn't say much during the drive. She had tried to comfort him, saying things like, "It's going to be okay" and "You're safe now," but Alex barely heard her. Her words seemed hollow, unable to reach the parts of him that had been shattered.

When they pulled up in front of the foster home, a modest house with a small porch, Alex felt his stomach twist into knots. His aunt and uncle hadn't wanted him back. They had made that clear. After everything he had been through, the people who were supposed to care for him had turned their backs. He was being left with strangers, people he didn't know and couldn't trust. The thought filled him with dread.

The car stopped, and the social worker glanced at him with a sad smile. "Here we are," she said, her voice gentle. "You'll be okay here, Alex."

Alex didn't respond. His throat felt tight, and his heart pounded in his chest as he looked at the house. He didn't know these people. He didn't know if they would be kind or if they would be just like everyone else—disappointed and angry with him. The fear of the unknown wrapped itself around him, suffocating him with anxiety.

The social worker opened the car door, but Alex stood momentarily frozen in his seat, staring at the house as if it were some prison. Eventually, he forced himself to move. He grabbed his small duffel bag from the back seat, the only belongings he had left, and stepped onto the sidewalk. His legs felt heavy, like he was walking through water, each step more complex than the last.

The social worker walked him to the porch, reassuringly squeezing his shoulder. "This is a good home," she said softly. They'll take care of you here."

But Alex wasn't so sure. He had heard those kinds of promises before, and they had always fallen short.

The front door opened, and a woman appeared, her face kind but cautious. She smiled, but Alex could see the hesitation behind her eyes, the uncertainty of what to do with a boy who had been through so much. She introduced herself as Mrs. Harris and welcomed him inside, but Alex barely heard her words. He felt detached from the world around him as if watching everything unfold from a distance.

As the social worker said her goodbyes and drove away, leaving him on the porch with Mrs. Harris and her husband standing behind her, a cold realization settled over Alex: he was alone again. The car disappearing down the street felt like the last connection to anything familiar, and now, once again, he was being dropped into the unknown, into a life he didn't understand, with people he didn't know.

He didn't know what to expect. He didn't know if this home would be different or if it would be just another place where he felt unwanted. All he knew was that the world he had once known—his family, his home, even the life he had tried to build on the streets was gone. Everything had been stripped away, leaving him feeling empty and lost.

Mrs. Harris stepped forward and placed a hand on his shoulder. "Come on inside, Alex. Let's get you settled in."

Alex nodded, his body moving on autopilot as he entered the house. The door closed behind him, shutting out the cold air, but the chill remained inside him, deep and unshakable. He was in a new place, but it didn't feel like home. It felt like another stop on a journey that had no end.

As he stood in the entryway, his bag hanging from his shoulder, all he could think was that he was alone. Truly alone. And he didn't know if he would ever feel anything else.

February 1st, 2004

To Alex's surprise, the foster home wasn't as bad as he had feared. After the pain and loneliness of the last few months, he had expected this new chapter in his life to be filled with the same emptiness he had grown accustomed to. But the moment he started interacting with the other kids, something shifted.

Several other children lived at the home, each with their own story and burdens. They weren't strangers for long. In a way, they became his family. Once intimidating and unfamiliar, the foster home walls soon became filled with laughter, whispered conversations, and shared stories late at night when they should have been sleeping.

The other kids welcomed Alex with a warmth he hadn't expected. They weren't just being nice out of pity; they truly understood what it meant to feel lost, shuffled from place to place, searching for something that felt like home. Alex was drawn into their circle, his guarded walls slowly coming down as they shared their stories with him. Some had been abandoned, others had lost parents to tragedy, and a few had fled homes filled with anger and neglect.

Hearing their stories made Alex realize something he hadn't allowed himself to feel in a long time—he wasn't alone anymore.

When it came time for Alex to share his story, he did so carefully. He talked about his father's death on 9/11, about how his mother had struggled with alcoholism, and how she had eventually taken her own life. He spoke about running away from his aunt's house, about how hard it had been living on the streets. But he left out the darkest part about the man under the overpass. That was something he couldn't share. Not yet. Maybe not ever.

Even without that piece of his story, the others listened, their eyes filled with understanding. They knew the weight of grief, the pain of losing the people you loved. And for the first time in a long time, Alex felt seen, truly seen. He wasn't just the boy who had survived terrible things; he was one of them, part of a group that understood his pain without judgment.

The days at the foster home passed quicker than he had imagined. There were rules and chores to do, but there was also a sense of routine, a structure that made him feel safe. The Harris family, who ran the home, were kind and patient, offering the kind of stability that Alex hadn't felt in years. They never pressured him to talk about things he wasn't ready to share, and they treated him with respect and made him feel valued.

At night, when the house was quiet and the other kids were asleep, Alex sometimes thought about his mother and father. He missed them both terribly, especially on the quiet nights when the memories would come rushing back. But even though the sadness was still there, it wasn't as crushing as it had once been.

Here, in the foster home, he had found a place where he could begin to heal, even if the wounds were still fresh.

He wasn't whole, he wasn't sure he ever would be—but he was happy in a way he hadn't expected. He had friends and people who cared about him, and for the first time since his world had fallen apart, he didn't feel completely lost.

As Alex lay in bed one night, staring at the ceiling, he realized something important: this foster home, this place that had once seemed so daunting, had become something close to home. It wasn't perfect, and it didn't fill the void left by his parents, but it was enough. For now, it was enough.

July 12th, 2008

After four years in foster care, Alex stood at the threshold of a new chapter in his life. He had just turned 18, and the world seemed to stretch before him, full of possibility and uncertainty. It was a moment he had been waiting for, yet it felt surreal now that it had arrived. The foster home that had once been a temporary refuge had become his home, and leaving it was bittersweet than he expected.

His foster parents, Mr. and Mrs. Harris, had helped him settle into his first apartment. It was a small place, nothing fancy, but it was his, and that was all that mattered. The apartment smelled like fresh paint and new beginnings, and as Alex stood there, looking around at the bare walls, he felt a sense of pride that he hadn't felt in a long time. This was his space, his life, and he had earned it.

Over the past four years, Alex had worked hard. He had learned the value of discipline and of pushing through challenges. He had grown from the scared, broken boy who had arrived at the foster home into a strong, capable young man. His foster father, Mr. Harris, had taken him under his wing, offering him more than just a roof over his head. He had given Alex the tools to survive in the world, literally and figuratively.

Alex had started working for Mr. Harris in construction when he was old enough. Over the years, Alex learned the trade.

He had become strong, his once thin and wiry frame filling with muscle from years of lifting, hammering, and building. The work was hard, but it gave Alex a sense of purpose, a feeling that he was creating something real with his hands. He enjoyed the rhythm of it—the sweat, the effort, the satisfaction of seeing a project come to life.

Mr. Harris hadn't just taught Alex how to work; he had also taught him how to fight. Growing up in foster care, Alex had dealt with his fair share of bullies, but Mr. Harris had made sure he would never have to feel powerless again. He showed Alex how to defend himself and stand his ground when necessary. They had spent hours sparring, boxing, and practicing self-defense to make Alex strong on the outside and give him the confidence to stand up for himself in all aspects of life.

In many ways, Mr. Harris had stepped into the role of the father Alex had lost. He had given Alex the guidance and skills his father had never had the chance to impart. And for that, Alex was deeply grateful.

Now, as he stood in his new apartment, Alex felt the weight of everything that had come before, both the pain and the growth. The foster system saved him, but the Harris family helped him heal. They had given him the tools to survive and build a future; now, it was up to him to make the most of it.

Alex ran his hand along the counter in the small kitchen, a smile tugging at the corner of his lips. The apartment was empty, but it didn't feel lonely. It felt like a beginning.

He looked out the window at the city beyond, the streets bustling with life. He had no idea what the future held, but Alex wasn't afraid for the first time in a long time. He was ready. He had strength in his hands, skills in his mind, and the support of the people who had become his family, even if they weren't tied to him by blood.

Alex knew his parents—his real parents—would never see the man he had become. They would never see him as strong, capable, and independent. But in his heart, he carried them with him. He carried on the lessons he had learned from the Harris family, who helped him rebuild his life when everything seemed lost.

Alex felt something shift inside as he closed the door to his new apartment behind him. He wasn't just surviving anymore. He was living.

December 25th, 2008

It was Alex's first Christmas with Kate, and although they had only been dating for a few months, it already felt like they had known each other for years. They had spent the entire day decorating the tree in her small apartment, laughing as they untangled lights and exchanged presents. The warmth between them was undeniable, and Alex couldn't remember the last time he had felt this connected to someone.

Kate made him feel safe, and the world seemed brighter, even on his darkest days. But no matter how much love he felt for her, Christmas still carried a shadow for Alex, one that lingered just beneath the surface. As they sat together on the couch, sipping hot chocolate and listening to Christmas music, Alex felt that familiar ache rise, pulling him back into memories he both cherished and dreaded.

He tried to focus on the present, the soft glow of the Christmas lights and the warmth of Kate's hand resting in his— but the pain was there, just below the surface, like a wound that had never fully healed. Christmas was once a magical time, filled with joy and laughter, back when his parents were still alive. His father had always made the holiday special, and his mother's laughter had filled their home with warmth. But those days were long gone, replaced by years of heartache and loss.

Alex's mind drifted back to those memories as the hours passed, and the sadness weighed on him. He remembered his last Christmas with his parents before everything fell apart. It had been a day much like this one, filled with love and warmth. But that life had been ripped away from him, leaving behind a hollow space that no amount of holiday cheer could ever fill.

Kate noticed the shift in his mood, her eyes softening as she touched his cheek. "Hey, what's wrong?" she asked gently, her voice full of concern.

Alex forced a smile, but it didn't quite reach his eyes. "Nothing... I'm just thinking."

Kate didn't press him, but she could see the sadness in his expression. "Is it about your parents?"

Alex nodded, his throat tightening as he struggled to find the words. "I miss them," he said quietly, his voice barely above a whisper. "I always miss them, but Christmas... Christmas makes it harder. It used to be my favorite time of year, and now... now it just reminds me of everything I lost."

Kate leaned closer, wrapping her arms around him in a comforting embrace. "I'm so sorry, Alex. I can't imagine how hard it must be."

He closed his eyes, trying to focus on her warmth and their love, but the memories wouldn't let him go. He could still see his mother, her face lighting up as she unwrapped presents, and his father's deep and joyful voice filling their home with laughter. Those memories were beautiful but also painful, a reminder of what he could never get back.

"I want to be happy," Alex admitted, his voice breaking. "I want to enjoy this day with you. But... I don't know how to separate the pain from the memories. I don't know how to let go."

Kate held him tighter, her hand gently stroking his back. "You don't have to let go," she said softly. "You don't have to push the pain away to be happy. It's okay to feel both. It's okay to miss them and still enjoy the present."

Her words soothed him in a way he hadn't expected. She wasn't trying to fix him or tell him to move on; she was reminding him that it was okay to feel everything and to let joy and sorrow exist side by side.

For the rest of the evening, they sat together in silence, the glow of the Christmas lights casting soft shadows on the walls. Alex's heart still ached for his parents, but for the first time in years, the weight of that grief didn't feel quite so overwhelming. He had Kate now, and although his past would always be a part of him, so was the life he built with her.

Christmas might never be the same, but that doesn't mean it couldn't be good again.

December 31st, 2008

Like many other New Year's Eve celebrations, his night started full of excitement, laughter, and anticipation for the year ahead. Alex began drinking early, wanting to let loose and forget about the weight of the past year. But as the hours passed and the alcohol flowed, that familiar darkness began to creep in, blurring the edges of his joy until it was replaced by something more destructive.

By the time midnight rolled around, Alex was drunk—far too drunk to think clearly. His head swam, and his emotions felt like they were teetering on a razor's edge, ready to spill over at any moment. It didn't take much for things to spiral out of control. A careless comment from another guy at the party, something that, on a typical night, Alex might have brushed off, set him off like a match to gasoline.

Before he knew it, Alex's fists were flying, and he was throwing punches. The guy fought back, but Alex was too far gone to care. The room erupted into chaos, people shouting, trying to pull them apart. But all Alex could feel was the heat of his anger, adrenaline rush, and the familiar, sickening release of losing control.

Through the haze of the fight, he caught glimpses of Kate, her face pale, her eyes wide with shock and fear. She stood frozen, helpless, watching her boyfriend become someone she barely recognized. But Alex was too deep into his rage and drunkenness to stop, even as the partygoers dragged him away, yelling at him to calm down.

Eventually, someone shoved him toward the door, and Alex was thrown out of the party. He stumbled down the street, still fuming, still too drunk to understand what had just happened. The cold night air bit at his skin, but it did little to sober him up. His mind was a blur of confusion and anger; all he wanted to do was get home.

When he finally reached the apartment, Kate was waiting for him, her arms crossed, her face a mixture of worry and frustration. "What the hell happened, Alex?" she demanded, her voice tight with emotion. "Why did you start that fight?"

Alex just shrugged her off, too drunk and ashamed to handle the conversation. "I don't know," he mumbled, pushing past her and heading for the bedroom. "Just... leave me alone."

Kate watched him, her heart breaking as he stumbled toward the bed, collapsing without another word. She didn't say anything else. There was no point in trying to talk to him when he was like this. All she could do was hope that, in the morning, he would realize the damage he had done.

When Alex woke the next day, his head was pounding, the dull throb of a hangover making him wince as he sat up in bed. His mouth was dry, his stomach queasy, and the events of the night before were nothing but a blur. He rubbed his temples, trying to piece together what had happened, but the memories were fragmented, hazy.

All he knew was that something had gone wrong. The feeling of shame settled over him like a heavy blanket as flashes of the fight came back to him, the shouting, the punches, the look on Kate's face as she watched him spiral out of control. He had messed up, big time.

Alex sat on the edge of the bed, his heart sinking as the weight of what he had done finally hit him. He had gotten too drunk, lost control, and hurt the people around him. And now, he had to face the consequences.

Kate was in the living room, sitting quietly with her arms wrapped around her knees. She didn't look up when Alex entered the room, but the tension in the air was thick, and Alex could feel her disappointment even before she said a word.

"I'm sorry," he said, his voice hoarse. "I don't know what happened last night."

Kate looked at him then, her eyes filled with hurt. "You started a fight, Alex. You scared me. You scared everyone."

Alex swallowed hard, the guilt gnawing at him. "I didn't mean to," he whispered. "I don't even remember... I just... I'm sorry, Kate. I'm so sorry."

She sighed, shaking her head. "You can't keep doing this. You can't just get drunk and lose control whenever something upsets you. I can't be around that. I won't."

Alex felt the sting of her words, but he knew she was right. He had a problem, one he couldn't keep ignoring. He had hurt the person he cared about most, and now, he was at risk of losing her. The thought terrified him.

"I'll make it right," he promised, his voice thick with emotion. "I don't want to lose you."

Kate didn't respond immediately, but after a long pause, she nodded. "We'll see," she said softly. "But something has to change, Alex. It must."

March 3rd, 2009

Alex paced the length of his small apartment, every step heavy with the weight of what he had just learned. Kate's words still echoed in his head: "I'm pregnant." It had hit him like a shockwave, reverberating through every part of his being, leaving him unsettled and unsure. He had been pacing for nearly an hour, his mind racing in circles, trying to process what this meant.

He stopped before the window, the dull gray city streets below offering no comfort. His breath fogged up the glass as he pressed his forehead against it, his heart hammering in his chest. Kate had been so calm when she told him it had almost felt surreal. He had expected panic, maybe even fear, but instead, she had looked at him with a quiet steadiness that had only amplified his internal chaos.

A baby.

The word itself seemed too big to fit into the world he knew. He had never imagined himself as a father. Hell, he could barely imagine himself as an adult most days. His life had been a string of bad decisions, missed opportunities, and relentless self-destruction. How was he supposed to bring a child into that? How was he supposed to be someone's father when he had felt lost and broken for so long?

And yet, beneath all the fear and doubt, there was something else—a flicker of light, a strange sense of hope that hadn't been there before. He didn't understand it entirely, but it grew slowly, quietly, in the corners of his heart.

He sank onto the couch, resting his head in his hands, his thoughts spiraling between the past and the future. He couldn't help but think about his childhood: the chaos, the pain, and the constant feeling of being unwanted. His father had disappeared when he was still too young to remember him, and his mother... she had been consumed by her demons long before Alex had even understood what was happening. He had been passed around, forgotten, and left to navigate life alone.

He had promised himself long ago that he would never become like them. He had sworn that he would be different if he ever had a family. But the years hadn't been kind, and he had slipped down the same path, letting addiction and anger rule his life. And now, with the news of Kate's pregnancy, the fear of becoming his father, of making the same mistakes, gnawed at him.

"What if I fail?" The thought echoed through him, sharp and relentless. *"What if I ruin this too?"* But then, as his mind raced, another thought broke through the haze, a quieter, softer one. *"What if I don't?"*

The possibility hung there, fragile and tentative but real. What if he could do better? What if this baby was the second chance he had always wanted but never believed he deserved? He didn't have to repeat the past. He didn't have to be the man his father was, the man his mother couldn't be. He could be something else, someone better. Someone his child could be proud of.

The idea was terrifying, but it was also exhilarating. For the first time in a long time, Alex allowed himself to imagine a future—one that wasn't defined by addiction or regret. He imagined holding his child for the first time, seeing their tiny face, and knowing that he was responsible for them, that their future depended on him. He imagined teaching them how to ride a bike, tucking them in at night, reading stories, and offering the kind of love and stability he had never known.

He imagined being there for them, showing up day after day, no matter how hard things got. He imagined a life without running from his past but building something better that would last.

The idea felt like a flicker of light in the darkness that had consumed him for so long. It wasn't a certainty. There were still so many questions and doubts, but it was hope. And that was something he hadn't felt in years.

Kate had told him everything would be okay, that they would figure it out together. And for the first time, Alex believed her. He had always loved her, but now, that love felt more profound, more meaningful. They were about to become parents, and the weight of that responsibility terrified him, but it also gave him something he hadn't had in a long time: purpose.

He leaned back against the couch, staring at the ceiling, letting it wash over him. There would be challenges, he knew that. His past wouldn't disappear overnight, and the road to becoming the kind of father he wanted to become would be difficult. But for the first time in his life, Alex wasn't afraid of the struggle. He was ready for it. He wanted to fight for this, for Kate, the baby, and himself.

He closed his eyes, imagining the child again—his child. The thought of meeting them, of seeing them grow, of being there for every milestone, every scraped knee, every tear, and every laugh filled him with a sense of resolve he hadn't known he possessed. This child was his second chance, his opportunity to break the cycle, to create something beautiful out of the wreckage of his life.

Alex opened his eyes and glanced at the clock on the wall. It was late, but the sense of urgency, the drive to do better, was stronger than ever. He picked up his phone, his fingers trembling slightly as he dialed Kate's number.

When she answered, her voice soft and tired, he didn't hesitate.

"I want to do this," Alex said, his voice steady. "I want to be a father. I want to be there for you, for the baby. I know I've messed up a lot, but I won't mess this up."

There was a pause on the other end of the line, and Alex's heart raced, but when Kate spoke, her voice was warm, filled with a quiet relief.

"I know, Alex," she said softly. "We'll figure it out."

For the first time in a long time, Alex believed that maybe, just maybe, they would.

May 14th, 2009

It had been one of those long, grueling days, filled with frustrations Alex couldn't shake. The sun had already set when he left work, his body sore and his mind restless. He needed a break to let off some steam, so he headed to the bar just down the street from his apartment without overthinking. It was supposed to be a quick stop, a chance to clear his head with a drink or two before heading home. But Alex hadn't counted on the way his emotions would spiral.

The first drink went down easy, the second even easier. Before long, Alex found himself talking to people around him, the tension of the day slipping away as the alcohol worked its way into his system. But his frustrations bubbled up in ways he couldn't control the longer he stayed. Something small, a comment, or a look set him off. It was just like New Year's Eve all over again. He didn't even know what triggered it, but suddenly, Alex was in a heated argument with a stranger, voices raised, fists clenched, and the fight came.

It escalated fast; punches were thrown before either knew what was happening. The bar erupted into chaos, people shouting, trying to pull them apart, but Alex was too far gone to stop himself. By the time the police arrived, the damage had already been done. Alex was arrested, handcuffed, and led out of the bar, his head spinning with regret and the cold realization of what he had done.

Sitting in the back of the police car, Alex felt a wave of devastation crash over him. He had never been in trouble with the law before. He wasn't the kind of guy to get arrested, yet he was facing jail time because he couldn't keep his anger in check. The gravity of the situation weighed on him heavily as the alcohol began to wear off, leaving behind only guilt and shame.

When Kate showed up to bail him out, the disappointment on her face was evident. She didn't even have to say anything for Alex to feel the full weight of his failure. But she didn't stay silent.

The moment they got home, Kate laid into him. She wasn't yelling, but her voice was sharp, every word cutting deeper than the one before.

"Alex, what were you thinking?" she asked, her eyes filled with frustration and concern. "You're going to be a father, and you're out getting drunk and getting into fights? You can't keep doing this! You have to grow up."

Alex sat on the edge of the couch, his head hanging low as he listened to her lecture him. He knew she was right—deep down—but hearing it from her stung. It wasn't just the disappointment in her voice; it was the realization that he had let her down, let himself down. He had wanted to be better, but he kept falling back into old patterns, letting his anger and frustration control him.

"I know, Kate," Alex said quietly, his voice heavy with regret. "I screwed up."

"You didn't just screw up, Alex. You could've gone to jail! What would've happened to us? To the baby? You need to start thinking about more than just yourself." She paused, her eyes searching for his. "I love you, but I can't do this if you keep making choices like this."

Her words hit him like a punch to the gut. He had been so focused on his problems and his feelings that he hadn't stopped to think about how his actions were affecting Kate or their unborn child. She was right. He couldn't keep acting like this, couldn't keep making these kinds of mistakes. He had responsibilities now, and the thought of losing Kate, of not being there for his child, terrified him.

"I'll do better," Alex whispered, looking at her sadly. "I swear, Kate. I don't want to lose you or the baby. I'll figure this out. I'll grow up."

Kate's face softened, but the worry didn't leave her eyes. "I hope so, Alex. I do. Because I need you to be the man I know you can be."

As she walked away, leaving Alex alone with his thoughts, the silence of the apartment felt heavy. The weight of the evening, of his actions, pressed down on him. He couldn't shake the shame of what he had done, the realization that he had almost lost everything.

Sitting there, Alex made a quiet promise to himself: He would be better for Kate, the baby, and himself. He had made too many mistakes; it was time to start making things right.

July 4th, 2009

The Fourth of July had started as a celebration, the streets filled with laughter, music, and fireworks. But now, all Alex could hear was the pounding of his heart in his ears, the rush of blood surging through his veins. He stood over the man, fists clenched, his breath ragged as the adrenaline pumped through his body. The man lay motionless on the hardwood floor, blood pooling beneath his head, staining the floorboards a deep, dark crimson. Alex had never felt this rage, this uncontrollable, all-consuming fury.

It had all happened so fast. One moment, Alex and Kate, five months pregnant, walked through the crowded room, trying to enjoy the party. The next, a stumbling drunk collided with Kate, knocking her to the ground as if she were nothing more than an obstacle in his path. Alex's first instinct was to reach for her and help her up, but then he saw how the man had just kept walking. No apology, no acknowledgment—nothing. It was like Kate didn't even matter.

That was the moment something inside Alex snapped. Before he knew it, he was on the man, fists flying, each punch fueled by the fear and anger that had been simmering beneath the surface for months. He wasn't just hitting the man for knocking Kate down. He was hitting him for every doubt, every fear, every moment of uncertainty that had haunted him since he found out he was going to be a father. The man had become the embodiment of everything Alex couldn't control, and he was taking it all out on him, one punch after another.

Kate's voice was in the background, pleading with him to stop, but Alex couldn't hear her. He was too far gone, too deep in a rage to care about anything else. It wasn't until the man stopped moving, until the blood started seeping across the floor, that Alex finally came back to himself.

He stood there, staring down at the man, his chest heaving as the reality of what he had done began to sink in. The man wasn't moving. His face was a mess of blood and bruises, and for a split second, Alex wondered if he had killed him. He stepped back, his fists trembling, the anger still bubbling beneath the surface. Regret washed over him, but it wasn't the regret he thought it would be. It wasn't regret for hitting the man; it was regret that he hadn't hit him harder.

The thought made Alex's stomach twist, but he couldn't shake it. He looked at Kate, who was standing nearby, her face pale and eyes wide with shock and fear. She had been yelling for him to stop, but he hadn't listened. He had let the anger take over, and now, the consequences lay at his feet, bleeding out on the wood floor.

Kate's hand rested protectively on her swollen belly, her expression mixed with disbelief and concern. "Alex, what have you done?" she whispered, her voice trembling.

Alex didn't answer. He couldn't. His mind was still racing, his body shaking from the adrenaline rush. He took another step back, his eyes locked on the man's still form, and then he turned and walked away. He didn't know where he was going, didn't know what would happen next, but he couldn't stay there any longer. The scene of carnage he had created was too much to face.

As he walked out of the room, the sounds of fireworks exploded in the night sky, echoing in the distance like a cruel reminder of the celebration that was supposed to be happening. But for Alex, the only thing that mattered now was the mess he had made and the fear that it would haunt him forever.

July 5th, 2009

The loud knock at the door startled Alex awake. His head pounded with the remnants of the night before, and for a moment, he wasn't sure if it had been a dream or if someone was there. Groggy and disoriented, he stumbled to his feet, the weight of the previous evening hanging over him like a dark cloud. His mind was hazy, but he knew something was wrong. He could feel it.

As he reached the door, Alex hesitated. He wasn't sure what or who he would find on the other side. The memory of the fight flickered through his mind, disjointed and blurry. He had beaten the man, that much he remembered, but the details were fuzzy, like a bad dream he couldn't quite piece together. Kate had tried to tell him what had happened, how severe it had been, but Alex had brushed her off. He hadn't wanted to hear it. He had convinced himself she was exaggerating and couldn't have been as bad as she said.

But as he opened the door, reality hit him like a punch. Two police officers stood on the other side, their expressions grim. Alex's stomach twisted in knots as he stepped back, the weight of their presence settling heavily on his chest. He knew why they were here, even if part of him had hoped he was wrong. His mind raced, trying to make sense of everything, but the officers didn't give him much time to think.

"Alex Stone?" one of them asked, his voice firm.

Alex nodded, his heart pounding in his chest. "Yeah, that's me."

"We're here to place you under arrest for assault and battery," the officer said, his tone cold and matter-of-fact. "The man you attacked last night is in critical condition. If his condition worsens, these charges could escalate."

The words hit Alex like a sledgehammer. "Critical condition?" He hadn't realized it had gotten that bad. The fight, the blood, and the rage felt distant, like something that had happened to someone else. But now, hearing it from the police, the gravity of the situation began to sink in. This wasn't just some bar fight. This was serious. Life-altering serious.

Before he could even react, the officers stepped forward, pulling his arms behind his back and slapping the cold metal handcuffs onto his wrists. The sharp click of the cuffs snapped him out of his daze, and suddenly, everything came rushing back. The blood, the man lying on the floor, and Kate's terrified voice begging him to stop it all crashed into him at once, and for the first time, he truly realized what he had done.

As the officers began reading him his rights, Alex's mind raced. He barely remembered how the fight had started, and now, the consequences were staring him in the face. The man was in the hospital, fighting for his life, and Alex was the one who had put him there. The thought made him sick to his stomach. How had he let it get this far? How had he lost control so completely?

Kate appeared in the doorway, her face pale and filled with fear and sorrow. She had warned him about the severity of the beating and had tried to tell him that it wasn't just a drunken scuffle, but Alex hadn't listened. He had refused to believe it, pushing her words away like they were part of a nightmare he could wake up from. But now, there was no escaping it.

"Kate..." Alex began, his voice hoarse, but she shook her head, tears welling in her eyes.

"They told me what happened," she whispered. "I tried to tell you... I didn't want this, Alex. I didn't want any of this."

Her words were a knife in his chest, cutting deep into the regret and shame that was already gnawing at him. Alex opened his mouth to apologize and say anything to make this right, but no words came out. He knew there was nothing he could say. The damage had been done.

As the officers led him toward the patrol car, Alex's heart sank lower with each step. The future he had been trying to build the future with Kate and their child seemed crumbling before his eyes. He had always feared becoming the kind of man his father had been, and now, standing on the edge of his destruction, he realized he had become someone even worse.

The car door slammed shut behind him, and as the officers pulled away, Alex leaned against the window, staring blankly at the world outside. Everything had spiraled out of control, and now he was facing a more uncertain future.

He had no idea how to fix this. He wasn't sure if he even could.

July 7th, 2009

Alex had always known how to fight. It was something he had learned out of necessity, not choice. Growing up, he had been the kid everyone picked on, the one who was pushed around and bullied. But after years of taking hits, he decided he wouldn't be anyone's punching bag anymore. His foster father had seen that fire in him and taught him how to channel it, defend himself, and throw a punch that counted. Once Alex learned how to fight, he promised himself that he would never back down again.

He wasn't the biggest guy, and he wasn't the strongest either, but he had learned to hold his own. Fighting became second nature, and after a while, the fear that used to grip him when fists flew turned into something else, something darker. Fighting became a way to prove he wasn't weak and keep control when everything else in his life felt like it was spiraling out of control.

That's why, on July 4th, when Kate was knocked down by that stumbling drunk, Alex didn't hesitate. He acted on instinct, on rage. Seeing her hit the ground had ignited something in him, something primal, and he had unleashed every bit of anger he had in him. He beat the man until he was motionless, his fists bruised and bloody. In the heat of the moment, it felt like justice, like protecting the woman he loved. But now, that fire had burned out, replaced by a cold, sinking dread.

The man hadn't just been injured. He was dead.

When Alex got the news, the floor had dropped from under him. The assault charge he had been facing had been escalated to manslaughter. The words hit him like a punch to the gut, harder than any blow he had ever taken in a fight. He had killed a man. It wasn't self-defense anymore; it wasn't just a brawl that got out of hand. A life had been taken, and Alex was the one who had taken it.

He hadn't meant to kill him. He wasn't a murderer. But that didn't change the fact that the man was dead because of him.

Alex sat in his cell, staring at the walls as the weight of it all pressed down on him. He could still hear Kate's voice, yelling at him to stop that night, begging him to walk away. But he hadn't listened. He had been too angry, too consumed by the need to protect her, to prove that no one could hurt her without facing the consequences. The man should have been more careful. He should have been more respectful. He shouldn't have knocked Kate down like she didn't matter.

As reality set in, Alex couldn't help but feel the crushing guilt. The fight had been about more than just that man. It had been about all the rage and frustration Alex had been carrying for years. It had been about the pain he never knew how to deal with, the anger that always seemed to simmer beneath the surface. He hadn't been fighting to defend Kate. He had been fighting to prove something to himself, the world, and anyone who doubted him. But now, that fight had cost a man his life.

The man's face flashed in his mind—bloodied and broken, and Alex felt sick to his stomach. He hadn't wanted this. He had never wanted to kill anyone. But what he wanted didn't matter anymore. The consequences of his actions were staring him in the face, and there was no escaping them.

His mind raced, trying to make sense of everything. What would happen now? What would Kate think of him? How would he face her knowing his anger had gone too far? And what about the baby? He had a family to think about now, a future that seemed to be slipping through his fingers.

As he sat there, lost in his thoughts, the reality of his actions began to sink in. He had killed a man, and no amount of regret could change that. The courts would decide his fate, but the guilt and the weight of that life he had taken would be something he would carry with him forever.

September 12th, 2009

Alex hadn't always been a fighter. In fact, for most of his childhood, he had been the one getting pushed around, the kid everyone picked on. But after years of bullying and feeling powerless, something had changed inside him. Losing his parents, moving from one foster home to the next, and constantly fighting to prove he wasn't weak—it had all shaped him into someone who wouldn't back down anymore. He had learned how to defend himself, how to stand his ground. Fighting became a part of him, a way to survive.

But now, as he sat in the courtroom, hearing the judge's words, it didn't feel like survival. It felt like defeat.

Alex had loved Kate and their unborn child more than anything, driving him to act without thinking. That night, when the drunk had knocked her down, something primal had taken over. He hadn't hesitated to beat the man, fueled by the fear of losing Kate and the anger that always seemed to simmer beneath the surface. He had meant to defend her, to make sure no one treated her that way, but the line between protection and rage had blurred.

He had taken a life. There was no changing that now. He had told himself it was an accident, that he hadn't meant to kill the man. But deep down, Alex knew he had let his anger take control. Maybe the alcohol had clouded his judgment; perhaps he had gone too far, but at the time, all he could see was someone who had disrespected the person he loved most. It didn't matter that the man had stumbled; it had been an accident. In Alex's mind, he had been defending Kate, even if it had cost him everything.

When the sentence of 10 years in prison came down, the weight of it hit him harder than any punch he had ever taken. Ten years. A decade of his life was gone. And the worst part was, Kate wasn't even there to hear it. She hadn't been in the courtroom at all. A month before the trial, she had left him, packed her things, and gone to live with her parents. He hadn't heard from her since.

The memory of her leaving still haunted him. She hadn't even said goodbye or given him a chance to explain or apologize. She had just disappeared, taking their unborn child with her. Alex had spent the past month wondering what she was thinking and feeling. He had hoped she would return and at least be there when he faced the judge, but she wasn't. The seat where she should have been empty, and that emptiness felt like a hole in his chest.

As the judge finished speaking, Alex felt numb. The words washed over him, distant and cold, like they were happening to someone else. Ten years. He could barely comprehend it. How had his life come to this? A fight, a moment of anger, had cost him everything: his freedom, family, and future.

The gavel struck, and it was over. The courtroom emptied around him, but Alex remained seated, staring blankly ahead. He didn't feel like a criminal. He didn't feel like a murderer. He felt like a victim, someone who had been pushed too far, someone who had lost control in a world that had always seemed out of his control.

The truth was, none of that mattered now. He had taken a life, and no amount of justification could change that. He would spend the next ten years behind bars, paying for that moment of rage. And Kate, Kate was gone, out of his life, leaving him to face this alone.

As the guards approached to take him away, Alex stood, his legs heavy with the weight of his sentence. The future stretched out before him, bleak and uncertain, and all he could do was walk forward into it, knowing that everything he had fought for was gone.

December 25th, 2009

Alex had never imagined spending Christmas behind bars. He had always pictured himself spending the holidays with Kate, their baby cradled in her arms, the warmth of a home filled with love and laughter. But that vision felt like a distant dream now. Instead, he sat alone in a cold, gray cell, the weight of the concrete walls pressing down on him as the sounds of other inmates echoed through the prison. They were celebrating together, exchanging jokes and stories, finding whatever joy they could in the bleakness of their surroundings. But Alex didn't feel like celebrating.

He couldn't escape the loneliness that gnawed at him, the hollow ache that had settled deep in his chest. The reality of where he was and where his life had led him hit harder today than any other day. Christmas used to mean family, warmth, and the promise of a new beginning. Now, it was just another reminder of what he had lost.

He sat on the edge of his narrow cot, staring at the faded walls, his thoughts drifting back to Kate. It had been months since he had heard from her—since before the trial when everything had still seemed salvageable. But after his arrest, she had vanished from his life, leaving him to face the consequences alone. She had made her decision: Alex wasn't worth waiting for. He wasn't worth the trouble, the pain, or the burden of his mistakes.

A few weeks ago, Alex had learned that Kate had given birth to a baby girl. She had named her Hannah. The news had come from a distant source, someone he barely knew, but it hit him like a punch to the gut. His daughter, "his" daughter, had been born, and he hadn't even been there. He would never see her first steps, never hear her first words. Kate hadn't even told him herself. Her silence had been deafening, final confirmation that she had moved on without him. And with that silence came the realization that he was, once again, utterly alone.

Alex leaned back against the cold wall, closing his eyes as the world's weight settled on his shoulders. His thoughts drifted to Hannah, his little girl, who would never know him and grow up without a father. He imagined her in Kate's arms, her tiny face full of innocence and wonder, utterly unaware of the broken man sitting in a prison cell, aching to know her.

It was hard to grasp how much had changed in such a short time. Last Christmas, he had been full of hope, thinking about the future he and Kate would build together. They had talked about the baby and their plans for a family. It seemed like things were finally coming together. But then came the fight, the anger, the night that had ruined everything. The cold, hard reality of bars and steel doors replaced that hope.

The other inmates continued their celebration, their laughter echoing through the halls, but Alex felt like he was on the outside, looking in. He didn't belong in their world, and he didn't belong in the life he had once envisioned, either. He was stuck in between, with no place to call his own.

As the hours passed and the light in his cell grew dim, Alex's mind wandered to all the Christmases he had spent with his parents before their deaths before the chaos of his life had taken over. He longed for that sense of belonging, of being part of something greater than himself. But now, it felt like those days were just ghosts, memories slipping further away each year.

Christmas in prison wasn't just another day; it was a reminder of everything he had lost, everything that could have been. As the sounds of celebration faded into the night, Alex was left alone in the silence, feeling more isolated than ever before.

April 17th, 2011

Alex had been in prison for over a year, and during that time, he had witnessed more violence than he thought possible. Fights broke out regularly, and the brutal reality of prison life had hardened him in ways he hadn't anticipated. He had learned to keep his head down, to stay out of trouble when he could, but there was no escaping the constant undercurrent of danger. He had seen men beaten within an inch of their lives, but nothing had prepared him for the night when he became the victim.

It started like any other night. The cell was cold, the lights dim, and the silence was unsettling. But then, without warning, his cellmates turned on him. They descended on him with fists and fury, and Alex could do nothing but try to defend himself as best as he could. But it wasn't enough. He wasn't strong enough. The blows rained down on him, hard and relentless, and the sharp pain of their fists and boots ripped through him. The concrete floor beneath him felt like ice, his body growing numb as the violence escalated. But the beating wasn't the worst part.

As he lay there, bruised and bloodied, they took it further. He had heard stories about this happening to others, but nothing could have prepared him for the horror of that moment. The feeling of being overpowered, of being completely helpless, consumed him. He tried to scream, but his voice caught in his throat, choked by the terror that gripped him. He felt his body break, felt the violation in every fiber of his being, and the pain was indescribable, physical, emotional, and soul-crushing.

The guards never came. Even if they had been watching, Alex knew they wouldn't intervene. In here, no one cared. He was alone, just another inmate, just another body.

By the time it was over, Alex lay motionless on the cold concrete, his body broken and bleeding. The silence that followed was suffocating, a stark contrast to the chaos that had just unfolded. His cellmates left him there, their footsteps fading into the distance, leaving Alex in a pool of his blood, feeling like he was dying.

He wasn't sure how he survived the night. Every breath felt like a battle, every movement a reminder of the horror he had endured. His mind raced, struggling to comprehend what had just happened, but the pain was too overwhelming. He wanted to give up, to close his eyes and never wake up again. But somehow, he held on. Deep inside, a tiny, flickering spark of survival remained, refusing to let go.

When morning finally came, Alex was barely conscious, his body stiff and aching, his wounds raw and exposed. The guards eventually found him and dragged him to the infirmary, but even in that sterile, fluorescent-lit room, there was no comfort. The nurses moved around him mechanically, treating his injuries without sympathy. In their eyes, he was just another inmate, just another case to deal with. There was no humanity here.

As he lay on the thin bed in the infirmary, staring up at the ceiling, the reality of his situation crashed down on him. He had survived, but at what cost? The person he had been, the man who had once loved Kate and dreamed of a future, felt like a distant memory. At that moment, Alex knew that prison hadn't just taken his freedom and everything. His sense of self, his dignity, his hope.

The physical wounds would heal, but the scars left behind by that night would never fade.

October 22nd, 2011

Alex had waited for this moment, the anger simmering inside him for months, slowly building until it was all he could feel. Every night since that terrible assault, he had replayed the events in his mind: the violence, the helplessness, the coldness of the concrete floor. He had vowed that he would never let that happen again. And now, his moment had come.

The satisfying crunch of bone echoed through the yard as his fist collided with the inmate's face. It was a sound Alex had dreamed of hearing, a release of all the rage festering inside him. He didn't hesitate. He didn't stop to think. His fists flew with a fury he hadn't known he possessed. Each punch felt like reclaiming something stolen from him, each blow a way to silence the voice in his head that had been screaming ever since that night.

The other inmates stepped back, their eyes wide with fear and shock. They knew better than to get involved. Alex wasn't the same man he had been when he entered this place, and the look in his eyes told them all they needed to know was that this wasn't a fight. It was vengeance. It was payback for what had been done to him.

His attacker, the man who had raped him, humiliated him, broken him, was on the ground now, but Alex didn't stop. The anger coursed through him like wildfire, his fists fueled by a rage that refused to be quenched. Blood spattered across the concrete with every punch, staining Alex's hands, but he didn't care. All he could see was the man beneath him, the man who had stolen his dignity, and Alex wasn't going to stop until that man felt every ounce of pain he had caused.

There was a sick satisfaction in each strike, a sense of power that Alex hadn't felt in a long time. He had been powerless for so long, first as a child, then in the streets, and finally in this prison. But now, for the first time, he felt in control. He felt invincible.

The man stopped moving long before Alex stopped hitting him. His face was a bloody mess, his body limp and lifeless, but Alex didn't care. He was lost in the violence, his knuckles cracking as they connected with bone, the feeling of flesh giving way under the force of his blows. Blood poured from the man's broken nose and mouth, pooling around his head, but Alex kept going, fueled by the fury of everything he had endured.

It wasn't until his own hands were slick with blood, his breath ragged, and his arms heavy that Alex finally stopped. He stood over the man's motionless body, his chest heaving, the adrenaline still pulsing through him. The inmate wasn't breathing. His chest didn't rise and fall, and his eyes stared blankly at the sky. Alex had beaten him to death, and yet, in that moment, all Alex felt was satisfaction.

He stood there, his fists bloodied and bruised, his knuckles raw, but there was no regret in his heart. No shame. This wasn't like the fight that had landed him in prison in the first place. This felt justified. This felt right. The man who had hurt him was gone, and Alex had been the one to end it. He had regained some of the control that had been ripped away.

The yard was silent now, the other inmates frozen in place, watching in stunned silence. The guards hadn't arrived yet, but Alex knew they would soon. It didn't matter. Nothing mattered now. He had done what he came to do.

As he stood over the lifeless body, the sense of triumph washed over him, mingled with the faintest hint of relief. He had done what he had promised himself he would do, and he had made the man pay. And Alex felt something close to peace for the first time in a long time.

As the guards' shouts echoed across the yard and the reality of what he had done began to sink in, Alex knew that this moment of satisfaction wouldn't last. There would be consequences—there always were—but he was okay with whatever came his way; he had no regrets.

October 24th, 2012

The metal clanging echoed through the prison corridors as the guards led Alex back to his cell. His wrists ached from the cuffs, but it was a slight discomfort compared to his deep chest satisfaction. Hours of questioning had ended, and Alex remained calm despite the accusations swirling around him. He had been accused of killing another inmate, the man who had raped him the year before, but the guards hadn't witnessed the fight. They only knew what everyone else in the prison knew: that the dead man had been one of the attackers. And now, he was gone.

Alex's fists clenched as the memories of that night flashed through his mind, fueling the anger that seemed to live inside him now, always simmering just below the surface. The guards had seen the inmate threaten him earlier and knew their history. It was no secret what had been done to Alex, and it seemed the guards had pieced together their version of events. They believed he had killed the inmate in self-defense, but without witnesses, there was no solid evidence to charge him. The warden had agreed, and the questioning had come to an end with no charges being pressed.

Alex wasn't sure why they hadn't pursued the case further, and he didn't care. The guards could do whatever they wanted; it didn't change the fact that the man who had violated him was dead. That was all that mattered. As they unlocked his cell and shoved him inside, Alex felt a dark satisfaction settle over him, a feeling that had been missing for far too long.

He lay back on the cold, hard bed, staring at the ceiling, his thoughts swirling. The dim light cast long shadows on the walls, but in his mind, everything was clear. The man who had haunted him and stripped away his dignity was gone forever, and Alex had played his part in making that happen.

He didn't care if he got caught; he wanted justice. He wanted the other inmates to see what would happen if they tried to mess with Alex Stone. He wanted to make a statement that resonated throughout the prison. He didn't want to do it where no one could see the carnage he inflicted. He wanted to show everyone what he was capable of.

The guards hadn't seen the fight, and no inmates wanted to get involved. They all said it was just a yard fight, and the prison couldn't make the charges stick without direct evidence. As far as they were concerned, another prison scuffle had gotten out of hand.

But Alex knew better. It hadn't been just another fight. It had been justice, his justice.

Since the incident, the other inmates have given him space. They kept their distance, eyes wary, whispers filling the air wherever he went. Everyone knows what happened, but no one dared confront him. In prison, respect is earned, often through violence, and Alex had just earned a reputation that would follow him for the rest of his sentence.

Lying on the bed, he let the satisfaction wash over him. It wasn't joy. Nothing had brought him joy in years, but it was close to peace. The rage that had consumed him for so long had finally found an outlet, and for the first time in what felt like an eternity, the anger wasn't bubbling over. The prison had paid for the rape he committed and for the one the guy in the alley had committed years ago when Alex was thirteen. Alex finally let both of those incidents go, and it felt good.

He knew that killing the man wouldn't undo the damage that had been done. It wouldn't erase the trauma, the violation, or the fear. But it gave him something, something he had been searching for since the day he was assaulted. It gave him power. Control. A feeling that he could take back what had been stolen from him.

The cell was quiet now, the distant sounds of prison life fading into the background. Alex closed his eyes, his hands resting on his chest, feeling the rise and fall of his breath. He wasn't a man who regretted much anymore. Regret was a weakness, and in prison, weakness got you killed.

The man who had hurt him was gone, and Alex could live with that. He didn't care why the guards hadn't pressed charges, and he didn't care what anyone else thought as long as they feared him, and they did. Inmates had seen fights before and even murders, but the rage and hate that showed on Alex's face they rarely saw. It wasn't a crazy look; it was a look of something else that could not be put into words. He had done what he needed to do. Now, all that was left was to wait out the rest of his sentence, knowing that the ghosts of his past were fewer than they had been before.

As Alex drifted to sleep, a grim satisfaction lingered in his mind, like a dark cloud that had finally lifted.

May 1st, 2013

Alex sat on the edge of his bed in the dimly lit prison cell, the cold concrete walls closing around him as always. He had been in this place for almost four years, and most days blended into a blur of monotony and regret. But today was different. Today, something had pierced through the fog of his existence, something he hadn't expected and shaken him to his core.

A letter had arrived that morning, one with handwriting he recognized immediately. It was from Kate, his ex-girlfriend, the mother of his child. For a moment, his heart had raced with a familiar mix of dread and hope as he carefully opened the envelope. He hadn't heard from her in so long, not since the few letters exchanged before the trial, and he had assumed she had moved on, built a life without him. He had always understood, though it didn't make it hurt any less.

But this letter—this letter was different. Inside was a photo, along with a few brief, carefully chosen words. It was a small, slightly crinkled photograph that Alex now held in his trembling hands. It was a picture of his daughter.

Alex's daughter was five years old now. He had never seen her before, not once. But there she was, in the photo, smiling brightly, her hair in soft curls, her eyes filled with joy. She was standing in what looked like a park, the sun shining down on her, casting a glow over her tiny frame. She seemed so happy, so full of life. And she was beautiful, so beautiful it hurt.

Alex's breath caught in his throat as he stared at the picture, his vision blurring with tears he hadn't expected. He had imagined this moment countless times, wondered what she looked like, how she was growing up, and whether she had any idea that her father even existed. And now, she was, captured in a precious moment, and it was almost too much to bear.

His daughter. His little girl.

Alex wiped his eyes with the back of his hand, overwhelmed by a wave of emotion that was equal parts joy and sorrow. He had missed it so much. He hadn't been there for her first steps, words, or day of school. He had been stuck in this place, paying for a mistake that had stolen his freedom and his chance to be a father.

But as he stared at the photo, something inside him shifted—a flicker of hope, a small but powerful sense of purpose. He wasn't too late. He could still be part of her life. He could still make things right.

Alex ran his thumb gently over the image, tracing the outline of his daughter's face. He felt a surge of determination rise in him, a feeling he hadn't experienced in a long time. He had messed up; he knew that. But this child, his child, was a reason to try again and fight for something better. She deserved a father, and he wanted to be that for her. Even if Kate had moved on and they could never be together again, maybe he could still have a place in his daughter's life.

The thought gave him a sense of hope he hadn't allowed himself to feel in years. The darkness that had consumed him, the guilt and the regret, felt a little less suffocating with the picture of his daughter in his hand. He wasn't just a prisoner anymore. He wasn't just a man who had made mistakes. He was a father.

With a deep breath, Alex pulled out a piece of paper and a pen. He wasn't sure what to say, but he knew he had to try. He had to write to Kate. He had to thank her for sending the photo and giving him this small but invaluable gift. And he had to tell her how much he wanted to be part of their daughter's life.

Alex's hand shook slightly as he began to write, but his resolve was firm. The words came slowly at first, but soon they flowed, filled with a raw, desperate honesty. He wrote about his regrets, missing out on their daughter's early years, and his hope for the future. He wanted to be better for his daughter, for himself.

Dear Kate,

Thank you for sending me the picture of our daughter. I don't even know where to begin. She's beautiful so much more than I ever could have imagined. I've stared at her picture for hours, trying to take in every detail, every part of her that I missed.

It's hard to say what it means to me to see her for the first time. But at the same time, it's a painful reminder of everything I've lost and missed because of my poor choices.

I know I haven't earned the right to ask you for anything, and I know I've let you down more times than I can count. I've made so many mistakes, and I've spent a long time thinking about the damage I caused to you, myself, and our daughter. There are no excuses for the choices I made. I put myself in situations that pulled me further from you and her, and I'm truly sorry for all of it. If I could go back and do things differently, I would, but I know that all I have now is the chance to do better moving forward.

I'm not writing this letter to try and erase the past. I know that's not possible. But I am writing to ask for a chance to be in my daughter's life when I am released. I know it won't be easy, and I don't expect things to change overnight. But I'm willing to put in the work to prove to you, and to her, that I can be the father she deserves.

I've thought about her every day since she was born, and even though I haven't been there, she's been the reason I've kept fighting to get better. I know that being part of her life will take time to earn your trust, show you that I've changed, and show her who I really am, not the man I was. I don't want to disrupt her life or push for something you're not ready for. All I'm asking for is a chance, even if it's limited. A chance to get to know her, to build something slowly, and to prove that I can be a good father if you're willing to give me that opportunity.

I understand that there's a lot of work ahead of me. I'm still in prison, and it's going to take time before I'm even able to be part of her life. But I've spent the last few years trying to turn things around and am committed to staying on this path. I want to show you that I'm not the man who ended up here. I've learned a lot and realized what matters most, my daughter. I know it will take time to rebuild trust, but I'm willing to do whatever it takes. I want to be there for her, even if that means starting small. I'll take whatever you're comfortable with, even if it's just letters or supervised visits when I'm released. I'll work with you, at your pace, to do what's best for her.

I know I can't make up for the years I've missed, and it will take time for you to believe I've changed. But I'm willing to be patient, to put in the effort, and to prove to you and our daughter that I can be the father she needs. I haven't been that man, but I want to be. More than anything.

I'm sorry, Kate. For everything. I'm sorry for the hurt I caused and for not being there for you or her when you both needed me. I can't undo the past, but I'm asking for a chance to make things right however I can. I hope you'll consider it. I promise you that I'm willing to do the work and take the time necessary to prove that I'm serious about this.

Thank you again for the picture. It means more to me than I can put into words.

Take care,

Alex

When he finished the letter, Alex sat back and stared at the photo once more. The image of his daughter filled him with a quiet sense of purpose. He wasn't sure what Kate would say or if she would even respond, but he had to try. This was his chance, maybe his only chance, to start building something good out of the wreckage of his life.

He carefully tucked the photo back into the envelope, his heart full of cautious hope. For the first time in a long time, Alex believed that maybe he wasn't too far gone. Maybe, with time, he could find redemption. Maybe, just maybe, he could be the father his daughter and Kate deserved.

August 13th, 2013

Alex paced his cell, his thoughts swirling in a chaotic storm. The news had hurt. Kate had married someone else. He had been a fool to think there was a possibility or chance for them to patch things up. He was happy for her, but it still made him sad.

The handful of letters between them had always been brief and distant, but he had clung to them, imagining there was still some connection, a chance that they could rebuild the life they had lost. But he should have known better. After all, he had been in prison for nearly four years. What could he have expected? Kate had every right to move on. She had their daughter to think about. Still, that knowledge didn't make the pain any easier to bear.

His pacing stopped as the weight of the truth settled in, heavy and suffocating. Alex sat down on the edge of the bed, burying his face in his hands. His mind was a whirlwind of regret, anger, and sorrow. He wondered how he would fit into his daughter's life now that she had a father, and Alex feared the place he would have with his daughter. He had heard that he was a good man and treated both well. He had no one to blame but himself.

Alex's thoughts drifted back to his choices—the fights, the reckless decisions, the anger that had consumed him. All of it had led him to this tiny cell, cut off from the world he had once been a part of. He had thrown away the best parts of his life, and now he was paying the price.

The news of Kate's marriage felt like a final, crushing blow. He had always known, deep down, that their relationship was long over, but part of him had stubbornly held on to the fantasy that, once he was released, they could start over. He had imagined showing up at her door, apologizing for everything, and somehow making things right. But now, that door was closed forever.

Alex lifted his head, staring blankly at the concrete walls surrounding him. He thought of his daughter, Hannah, and the picture Kate had sent him months earlier. She was growing up without him, and now, she had another man in her life, someone who would be the father Alex could never be. That thought stung him the most. He had failed not only Kate but his daughter, and there was no way to fix it. No way to turn back time.

The realization that he was alone settled over him like a cold, heavy blanket. He had spent so much of his life fighting against bullies, his demons, against the world.

As he sat there, the silence of the cell pressing in on him, Alex knew that the hope he had been holding on to was gone. He had lost everything that mattered, and there was no getting it back. Kate had moved on. Hannah would possibly never know him. And he would remain behind bars, serving time for the mistakes that had cost him everything.

With a deep sigh, Alex lay back on the bed, staring again at the ceiling. The future stretched out before him, bleak and empty, and for the first time, he couldn't imagine what it would look like. All the dreams he had held on to had slipped through his fingers, leaving him with nothing but the cold reality of what his life had become.

January 27th, 2014

Alex had been dreading this day for weeks, though part of him tried not to admit it; his parole hearing was approaching, and he feared being rejected again. From the moment the date was set, he had known that his chances of being released were slim, but the thought of trying to stand in front of the parole board and making his case was enough to stir up hope, no matter how faint it was. He hoped that maybe, just maybe, this would be the day he could leave this place behind.

He sat in the waiting room, his leg bouncing nervously as the minutes dragged on. The walls around him felt too close and oppressive, and his mind raced with thoughts of what he could say and do to convince the panel that he deserved to be released. He thought of all the things he would miss if they sent him back to his cell: the simple pleasures he hadn't experienced in years. He was walking in the park, feeling the sun on his face, hearing the wind in the trees. The idea of freedom, of a life outside these walls, seemed like a dream that had grown distant and hazy during his years of incarceration, but now, the possibility of that dream felt close enough to touch, even if only for a moment.

Alex's hands were slick with sweat, and he wiped them on his pants as he tried to steady his nerves. He knew the odds weren't in his favor. He had a violent past, a record that spoke louder than any words he could offer. But still, he had to try. He had to believe that maybe there was a way out of this.

The door opened, and Alex's heart skipped a beat. A guard stepped inside, calling his name. "Stone, you're up."

Alex took a deep breath, standing up on shaky legs. He followed the guard down the hallway, his mind buzzing with anxiety. The closer he got to the hearing room, the harder it became to control his racing thoughts. What could he say? How could he prove that he had changed and wasn't the man who landed himself here almost five years ago?

When he stepped into the room, the air was heavy with tension. The parole board sat before him, their faces impassive, their expressions unreadable. Alex felt a knot tighten in his stomach as he took his seat. His hands fidgeted in his lap, his gaze flicking between the board members as they began the hearing.

Questions were asked about his behavior in prison, the programs he had participated in, and his plans if he were released. Alex answered as best he could, his voice steady but his heart pounding. He spoke about his regrets, the things he had learned, and his desire to make things right. He tried to convey the depth of his remorse, the weight of his mistakes, and the man he wanted to be outside these walls, but deep down, he could feel it slipping away. The board members listened, but their faces remained unchanged, unmoved.

And then, after what felt like an eternity, the decision came.

"Parole denied."

The words echoed in Alex's mind, sharp and final. His breath caught in his throat, and for a moment, he couldn't move. It was over. The hope he had clung to, fragile and flickering, was gone instantly. The reality of his situation crashed down on him like a wave, cold and unforgiving; he had failed.

As he stood up, his legs felt heavy, as though they could barely carry him. The guard motioned for him to follow, but Alex hesitated for just a moment, letting the weight of the decision sink in. He wasn't going anywhere. Not today. Not for a long time.

The walk back to his cell felt longer than it ever had before. The prison noise faded into the background. All he could think about was what he would miss, the things he had lost, and the future that had slipped through his fingers.

Alex buried his face in his hands as he sat on his bed. He had known, deep down, that his chances were slim. But knowing it didn't make the rejection any easier. He was still trapped in the life he had built for himself, and there was no escape.

May 23rd, 2014

Four months had passed since Alex's parole had been denied, and with each passing day, the weight of that decision pressed down on him more. Once, a small flickering light in the dark, Hope had been completely snuffed out. He had spent those months trying to hold on and convince himself that there was still something worth fighting for, but the emptiness inside him grew too large to ignore. The pain, the regret, and endless despair became too much.

The drugs had always been there, in the shadows of the prison, whispered about in hushed tones and exchanged in secret. Alex had resisted their pull for a while, telling himself he wouldn't fall into that trap. But after the parole hearing, something inside him broke. The voice in his head that used to say "Just hold on" went quiet, replaced by the loud, relentless call for escape, so he gave in.

It started with heroin, a drug that promised to numb the pain, to make everything go away, at least for a little while. Alex injected it into his veins, and the constant ache in his chest disappeared for the first time in months. The sadness, guilt, and crushing weight of his failures all melted away, leaving behind a comforting numbness. He didn't feel happy, but he didn't feel sad either. At that moment, he felt nothing seemed like the best he could hope for.

Cocaine followed not long after, a different kind of high, one that made him feel alive in a way he hadn't in years. The rush coursed through his veins, making the prison walls blur and fade, making him forget that he was trapped in this place. For a moment, he felt invincible, like he could escape the reality of his life, even if only in his mind. But the high never lasted long. It would always wear off, leaving him right back where he had started, empty, broken, and alone.

The cycle began to repeat itself, day after day, week after week. Alex would use, chase the high, feel nothing, and then crash back into the same dark pit he had been trying to escape. And then he'd use it again, desperate for that brief reprieve. He knew he was spiraling, that the drugs were becoming more than just an escape. They were becoming a need, an addiction he couldn't shake. But the truth was, he didn't care. The thought of trying to fight his way out of this felt impossible, so he stopped trying altogether.

In prison, addiction was just another way to cope with the endless days and nights. Alex wasn't the only one who had given in to the lure of drugs, but that didn't make it any less destructive. The once-strong man who had fought to survive and dreamed of a life outside these walls was fading away, replaced by someone who just wanted to feel nothing.

The guards and the other inmates saw it, but no one said anything. This was a prison, after all. Everyone was fighting their own battles, and Alex's descent into addiction was just another story in the endless list of broken lives inside these walls.

His days blurred together, the sharp lines of reality dulled by the constant haze of drugs. His body grew weaker, his mind more clouded. He no longer thought about Kate or his daughter. He no longer cared about the life he had imagined outside of prison. He only cared about the next fix and escape from the suffocating emptiness.

There were moments, brief flickers of clarity, when Alex would look at himself and feel a pang of regret. He would remember who he used to be, what he used to want, and wonder how he had ended up here. But those moments never lasted long. The drugs would take over again, pulling him back into the numbness that had become his only refuge.

There seemed to be no way out, which was fine for Alex. He didn't want a way out anymore. He had lost everything that mattered, and now, he had lost himself too.

September 23rd, 2014

Alex winced in pain as he looked down at his hand, a deep gash cutting across his palm. The knife had slipped while he was working in the prison shop, and now blood was pouring from the wound, quickly soaking through his shirt. The sharp sting radiated up his arm, but the sight of the blood made his heart race more than the pain. He knew he needed help and fast.

The other inmates in the shop stopped what they were doing and gathered around to see what had happened. Some whispered, while others just stared at the growing pool of blood on the floor. But amid the commotion, one man stepped forward with a sense of calm and control.

"Sit down," said Tim, a grizzled convict who had been in and out of prison for most of his adult life. Tim had a reputation for handling challenging situations, and this one seemed no different to him. His eyes flicked from Alex's wound to the worried faces of the other inmates, and without hesitation, he took charge.

Alex, feeling lightheaded from the blood loss, did as he was told, lowering himself onto a nearby bench. Tim crouched beside him, quickly assessing the injury. "It's deep, but we can stop the bleeding," he said in a low, steady voice. Without waiting for a response, he pulled a bandana from his pocket, tying it tightly around Alex's hand to stem blood flow. The pressure hurt, but it was better than watching his lifeblood drain out.

"Keep that hand elevated," Tim instructed, motioning for one of the nearby guards. The guard, wary but trusting of Tim's knowledge in these matters, gave a nod, allowing him to help Alex to the infirmary. Tim firmly touched Alex's shoulder and guided him to his feet. "Let's get you patched up."

As they made their way to the infirmary, Alex's mind drifted, the pain and dizziness blurring the edges of his thoughts. He barely registered the curious looks of the other inmates as they passed, his focus narrowing to the ache in his hand and the warmth of the blood that continued to seep through the makeshift bandage. But through it all, Tim remained calm and steady, reassuring in the chaos.

Tim had seen more than his fair share of injuries in prison. He knew how things worked here and how to keep things from getting worse before they got better. As they approached the infirmary, Tim gave Alex a slight nod. "You'll be all right; you just need some stitches."

Alex, grateful but still in shock, managed a weak smile. "Thanks, Tim."

"Don't mention it," Tim replied, his expression unreadable. "We're all just trying to survive in here."

Once inside the infirmary, the medical staff took over, and Tim stepped back, fading into the background as quickly as he had come forward to help. Alex sat on the examination table, his hand throbbing, but his mind was clearer now that the immediate danger had passed. The nurse worked quickly, cleaning the wound and stitching it up, but Alex's thoughts kept drifting back to Tim.

In a place where survival often meant looking out for yourself, finding someone to help without hesitation was rare. Tim, despite his gruff exterior, had been that someone today. Alex didn't know much about him, but at that moment, he felt a strange sense of gratitude, not just for the help but for the unexpected humanity in a place that often felt devoid of it.

As the nurse finished up and Alex looked down at the neat row of stitches in his hand, he realized how close he had come to something far worse. And for the first time in a long while, he felt like maybe, just maybe, he wasn't entirely alone in this place.

January 29th, 2015

Alex paced the length of his cell, the anxiety bubbling inside him. His heart raced, every step feeling heavier than the last as the clock ticked closer to the parole hearing that would decide his future. It wasn't his first time in this position, but today felt different. The stakes were higher, the fear more palpable. This was his chance to regain his freedom, start over, and rebuild the shattered pieces of his life. But what if they said no?

The thought hung over him like a dark cloud. He had been here a year before, and that rejection nearly broke him. It had sent him spiraling into drugs and darkness, his hope crushed beneath the weight of his guilt. And now, he was again pacing the same small space, haunted by the same fear. What if it happened again? What if he wasn't ready? Tim had helped him kick the drugs, but he feared if he was denied parole this time, he might start again.

His mind raced through the last five years since he entered the prison. He thought about the fights, the mistakes, the moments of regret. He had killed someone in a moment of uncontrollable rage and, for that, landed him in this prison. But Alex had taken responsibility for his actions. Since then, he had spent every day trying to make sense of the man he had become and trying to change. He had done the work, participated in the programs, and talked to the counselors, but he knew that none of it would matter if the parole board didn't believe he was genuinely remorseful.

Alex knew the weight of his mistake, which he carried daily. He wanted to make up for it. He tried to live a life that would prove he wasn't just the man who had acted in anger. He wanted to be better. He wanted to be free.

Finally, the moment arrived. The guard appeared at his cell, and Alex's stomach twisted as he was led to the hearing room. His palms were slick with sweat, his breath shallow, but he forced himself to stay calm. This was his chance to show them who he had become and his chance at redemption.

The room was cold and sterile, the tension thick as the parole board entered and took their seats. Alex stood before them, feeling small and exposed, as if every detail of his life was being weighed and measured. The board members shuffled their papers, their expressions unreadable as they prepared to make a decision that would alter the course of his life.

Alex answered their questions as best he could, his voice steady despite the nerves pulsing. He spoke about his regret, his remorse. He talked about the programs he had completed and the time he had spent reflecting on his past. He told them about his hopes for the future, how he wanted to rebuild his life, and how he wanted to find a way to contribute to the world outside these prison walls. But most of all, he asked for a second chance.

The minutes dragged on like hours, each question heavier than the last. Finally, after what felt like an eternity, the board members exchanged a few quiet words before turning back to Alex.

"Parole granted."

The words hit Alex like a shock, disbelief washing over him. He had been preparing for rejection for the familiar crushing blow of "no." But now, the words "parole granted" echoed in his mind, almost surreal. He could barely process what it meant: freedom, a new beginning, and a chance to leave the past behind.

The room seemed to blur around him as he took in the reality of what had just happened. After all the years, all the regret, all the nights spent wondering if he would ever have a future beyond these walls, he was going to be free. He could hardly believe it.

As the guards led him out of the room, his mind swirled with thoughts of the future. It wouldn't be easy, he knew that. The road ahead was uncertain, and he would have to face the consequences of his past every day. But now, he had the chance to rebuild, make amends, and start over. It was more than he had dared to hope for. He had been given a second chance. And this time, Alex wasn't going to waste it.

March 14th, 2015

Alex stepped through the prison gates and into the sunlight, blinking against the sudden brightness. For a moment, he just stood there, feeling the warmth of the sun on his skin, a sensation he hadn't truly felt in over five years. The air outside was different, fresh, and full of possibilities, yet it also carried the weight of the unknown. Alex took a deep breath, his heart pounding as he looked at the world stretching out before him. This was freedom, but it was also terrifying.

The last five years had been brutal. He had survived the violence, the isolation, the crushing despair, and he had fought his way through the darkest parts of himself. But not all the battles had been won. In prison, he had turned to heroin to numb the pain, to escape the reality of who he had become. For the past year, the drug had controlled him and offered him an escape when there was nothing else. Now that he was out, he knew it would be his biggest challenge: staying clean and free.

Alex stared at the road ahead, feeling the weight of everything he had lost pressing down on him. He had no money, home, or family waiting for him. Kate had moved on, his daughter a distant memory he barely had the right to think about. But despite the emptiness, despite the odds stacked against him, there was something inside Alex that hadn't died his will to survive. He had made it this far and wouldn't give up now.

He started walking down the street, his footsteps slow and deliberate as he took in the sights and sounds of the world outside. The city bustled around him, cars rushing past, people moving with purpose. For Alex, everything felt new, overwhelming, and unfamiliar. He had been a part of this world once, but now it felt foreign like he didn't quite belong. But he knew that he had to find his place again to rebuild his life.

The addiction clawed at him even now, the familiar craving whispering in the back of his mind, urging him to find a fix. But Alex clenched his fists, determined to fight it. He knew that if he gave in, it would only lead him back to the same place he had just escaped, back to prison and the darkness. He couldn't afford to slip. He had been given a second chance, and he wasn't about to let it slip through his fingers.

The road ahead wouldn't be easy. He had no idea where to start. No job was waiting for him, no shelter to call his own. He didn't even know where he would sleep tonight. The reality of his situation was stark, but Alex didn't let it overwhelm him. He had spent too long giving in to hopelessness. Now, he had to fight for every step.

He walked for hours, eyes scanning the streets for any sign of opportunity. He thought about heading to a shelter, maybe asking around for work, anything that would get him through the next few days. He wasn't picky. He couldn't afford to be. What mattered now was staying clean, finding something to hold on to before the weight of the world crushed him.

Alex reminded himself of why he had to keep going with each step. He wasn't just walking away from prison. He was walking toward a life he had to rebuild from the ground up. And it wouldn't happen overnight. But if he could survive prison, if he could survive the addiction that had nearly destroyed him, he could survive this, too.

As the sun began to set and the shadows stretched longer on the pavement, Alex found himself at a crossroads, figuratively and literally. He had a choice to make. The road ahead would be challenging, but it was a chance. A chance to reclaim the life he had lost, to find purpose again. And he was ready to face it no matter how tough it would get. Because this time, Alex wasn't just surviving. He was fighting for his future.

March 28th, 2015

When Alex was released from prison, he clung to the hope that things would finally turn around. He had spent five years behind bars, paying for his mistakes, and now that he was out, he was determined to rebuild his life. But two weeks into his newfound freedom, the harsh reality of the outside world hit him harder than he expected.

Finding a job as a convicted felon wasn't easy. Every day, he pounded the pavement, searching for work, but no one was willing to take a chance on him. The jobs he did find, mostly day labor, were barely enough to cover his basic needs, including the weekly rent for the tiny apartment he had managed to scrape together. The bills were piling up, and each passing day brought a growing sense of desperation. The hope that had carried him out of prison was starting to fade, replaced by the cold fear that he might never truly escape the shadows of his past.

In this state of desperation, Alex found himself standing on the porch of his foster father's house, a place he hadn't been in years. His foster father had taken him in as a teenager, taught him the value of hard work, and given him the tools to survive. He ran a small construction company, and Alex knew the business inside and out. If anyone could give him a break, the man had once been like a father to him.

When his foster father opened the door, there was a moment of awkward silence between them, the weight of their shared history hanging in the air. Alex hadn't seen him in a long time, but there was a flicker of hope in his chest as he explained his situation. He told his foster father about his struggles to find steady work, about the day labor jobs that weren't enough to make ends meet, and then asked for a job. He knew the construction business well. He had worked for him as a teenager, and indeed, there had to be something he could do to help.

But as his foster father listened, the expression on his face told Alex everything he needed to know before he even said a word.

"I'm sorry, Alex," he said, his voice heavy with regret. "I just don't have enough work right now. And with your criminal record, my insurance won't cover you. I wish I could help, but my hands are tied."

Alex stood there, the words hitting him like a blow. He had hoped, maybe even expected, that his foster father would help him out, that he would be willing to take a chance on him when no one else would. But now, that hope was gone, replaced by the cold sting of rejection. His foster father wasn't turning him away out of malice. Alex could see that, but it didn't make the disappointment easier to swallow.

He nodded slowly, his heart sinking as he forced a smile. "I understand," he muttered, though the words felt hollow. "Thanks anyway."

His foster father touched his shoulder, offering a brief, awkward squeeze. "You'll figure something out, Alex. You've always been a survivor."

Alex didn't feel like a survivor. As he walked away from the house, the weight of his situation pressed down on him harder than ever. He was running out of options, running out of hope. He had been doing everything right, staying clean, trying to find work—but the world wasn't making it easy. No matter how hard he tried to move forward, the past kept dragging him back.

He felt lost, adrift in a world that seemed unwilling to give him a second chance. Every door he knocked on seemed to slam shut, and the few opportunities he found weren't enough to keep him afloat. The desperation gnawed at him, whispering in the back of his mind, tempting him to give up. But he couldn't. He had come too far to turn back now.

Still, as he walked down the street, his mind raced, trying to figure out what to do next. The world felt like it was closing in on him, and he wasn't sure how much longer he could hold on.

April 16th, 2015

A month had passed since Alex walked out of the prison gates, and every day since, there had been a battle against a world that seemed determined to keep him down. He had tried everything. Restaurants, retail stores, and construction companies. He had filled out application after application and made call after call, but the answer was the same each time. No one wanted to hire a man with a felony on his record. The door to a fresh start, which he had hoped for, seemed permanently locked.

The rejection wore on him. It chipped away at the fragile hope he had held onto when he was released. He had been determined to make a better life for himself, but now, that determination was fading fast, replaced by desperation. He couldn't escape. The rent was overdue, the bills were piling up, and the few dollars he had managed to scrape together doing day labor jobs weren't enough to keep him afloat.

It felt like the world was closing in on him, and with every passing day, the walls of his life got a little tighter. The pressure to survive became unbearable, and soon, Alex found himself standing at a crossroads he had hoped to avoid.

With no money, job, or one willing to give him a chance, he started slipping back into old habits. The streets had always provided an easy way out, and though he had vowed to leave that life behind, the allure of quick money became impossible to ignore. He knew it was risky, but what choice did he have? Starve? Become homeless?

The thought of going back to prison gnawed at him, but the fear of going hungry, of losing what little he had managed to secure since getting out, felt more immediate. He justified it to himself; it would be just one burglary, just a few drug deals, just enough to get by until he could figure something else out. But deep down, Alex knew where this road led.

He was out on the streets at night again, slipping through the shadows, casing houses, and making deals with people who wouldn't think twice about turning on him. Every burglary and every drug sale brought a fresh surge of adrenaline and fear. He told himself it was only temporary, that he'd find a way out soon. But it became harder to see a way back each time he walked away with cash in his pocket.

The streets were ruthless, the danger was always present, and Alex knew he was walking a tightrope, one wrong step away from falling back into the same pit he had barely crawled out of. But what was the alternative? He had tried playing by the rules. He had tried to do everything right, but the world didn't care. No one cared.

As the days passed, Alex sank deeper into the life he had sworn he wouldn't do. The desperation that had driven him to a life of crime. It was like a weight, pulling him under, and each time he closed a deal or hit another house, the guilt gnawed at him a little more. But the money was a necessity he couldn't deny.

He knew it was only a matter of time before things went wrong. He had seen people here before, and the outcome was never good. But for now, Alex didn't see any other choice. This was survival; survival was all that mattered in a world that had refused to give him a second chance.

May 22nd, 2015

Alex had been out of prison for a couple of months, trying to piece his life back together, but one thing gnawed at him more than anything else: the thought of his daughter. He had never seen her in person, and the ache of not knowing her and not being part of her life weighed on him daily. He had reached out to Kate, his child's mother, countless times, asking for a chance to meet his daughter and be part of her life in some way. But the answer was the same every time: "No, not yet, you just got out."

Alex couldn't understand why Kate was being so stubborn. He knew he had made mistakes, but prison had changed him, or at least, he was trying to change. He wasn't the same man he had been when he went in. He just wanted to know his child and be there for her in some capacity. But Kate wasn't budging.

Frustration bubbled inside him, and finally, Alex decided to take matters into his own hands. He couldn't just sit by and wait any longer. He needed to see Kate, to talk to her in person, to make her understand that he was serious about wanting to be part of their daughter's life. So, one afternoon, he went to her workplace, determined to discuss things face-to-face.

When Alex arrived, he stood in the background, watching from a distance. He saw Kate interacting with her co-workers, laughing and chatting easily, and for a moment, he felt a flicker of relief. She seemed happy as if she was doing well, which pleased him. Despite everything that had happened between them, it was good to see her thriving. Maybe, he thought, that happiness would soften her heart, make her more willing to let him into their daughter's life. But everything changed as the workday ended, and Kate headed to her car.

When she stepped outside and saw Alex waiting for her, the look on her face wasn't the relief or understanding he had hoped for. It was apprehension and possibly fear. Her eyes widened, her body tensed, and for a moment, she looked like she was ready to run. The tension between them was palpable, and Alex realized how much his presence unnerved her. But he wasn't there to scare her. He just wanted to talk.

"Kate," he said, holding his hands up in peace. "I just want to see my daughter. That's all. I'm not here to cause any trouble. I need to talk to her."

Kate's face hardened, her fear quickly shifting to anger. "You need to leave, Alex," she said, her voice tight. "I've already told you no. I'm glad you're out, but you need to get some time under your belt before you can see her. Show me that you have got your shit together, and we can talk about it then. You can't just show up here."

Alex took a step closer, desperate to make her understand. "I've changed, Kate. I've paid for my mistakes. I want the chance to be a father to her. I want to know my child."

Kate wasn't hearing any of it. Her hand tightened around her car keys, and her voice grew sharper. "No, Alex. I don't want you around her until you have changed. I don't want you in our lives yet. If you don't leave right now, I'll call your probation officer and report you."

The words felt like a slap. He stood there, stunned, as the weight of her rejection settled over him. He thought seeing her in person and talking to her face-to-face might change things. But now, it was clear Kate wouldn't let him back into their lives. She was saying later after some time, but Alex knew she meant never. No matter how hard he tried or how much he wanted to be a part of his daughter's world, Kate wouldn't budge.

For a moment, Alex's frustration flared. He had been patient and had tried to do things the right way, but now it felt like everything was slipping through his fingers. But as he looked into Kate's eyes and saw the fear and anger etched into her face, he knew he had no choice. Pushing further would only make things worse.

"I'm sorry," Alex muttered, his voice hollow. "I didn't mean to scare you or force you into a decision. I'll give it more time."

Kate didn't respond. She turned, got into her car, and drove away, leaving Alex in the parking lot, feeling more lost than ever. As the sound of her car faded into the distance, he realized that the future he had imagined, where he could be a father to his daughter, was slipping further out of reach. Once again, Alex stood at a crossroads, unsure of where to turn next.

June 23rd, 2015

Alex staggered down the dark alley, his vision blurring as the drugs coursed through his veins. The world around him tilted and spun, the dingy brick walls of the alley seeming to close in on him, making everything feel tight and suffocating. But the high, oh, the high, made it all feel distant. The euphoria had him floating, the numbness a welcome reprieve from the harsh reality of his life. He fumbled in his pocket, fingers trembling as they closed around the vial. All he wanted was another hit, just enough to keep the pain at bay, just enough to forget, at least for a little while.

As he pulled the vial from his pocket, he felt a sudden, sharp pain tear through his arm. The shock of it pierced through the fog of drugs, jolting him back to the harshness of the present moment. He gasped, his eyes darting down to see blood seeping through his shirt, dark and wet. He had been stabbed.

The realization was startling, adrenaline mixing with the lingering effects of the drugs, sending his heart racing. The vial slipped from his trembling hands, clattering to the ground as he tried vainly to stop the flowing blood. His hands pressed against the wound, but the blood kept coming, soaking his clothes and staining the alley floor. His breath grew ragged, and his knees buckled beneath him.

Alex collapsed to the ground, whimpering in pain, his mind spinning. This wasn't supposed to happen, not like this. He could barely think, barely breathe, the world spinning around him as the pain radiated through his body, and then he heard their footsteps.

Slow and deliberate, each step grew louder and more distinct until they finally stopped above him. Alex looked up, his vision hazy, his heart pounding in his chest. The figure that loomed over him was little more than a shadow, dark and menacing, blurred at the edges by the drugs that still pulsed through Alex's veins. But the coldness in the air, the malice he could feel radiating from the figure, made his blood run cold.

Alex tried to speak and plead, but the words wouldn't come. His mouth moved, but nothing came out. His body was too weak, too broken, to fight back. He could only watch as the figure leaned down, just close enough for Alex to make out the cruel sneer on the man's face, and then, without a word, the man's boot swung forward and connected with Alex's face. The force of the kick sent a jolt of pain through his skull, and in an instant, everything went black.

June 24th, 2015

Alex woke up in the hospital bed, dizzy and disoriented, the sterile smell of disinfectant filling his nostrils. His body felt heavy, like he was sinking into the mattress. His head pounded, and his vision swam as he tried to understand where he was. Slowly, the fog began to lift, and the bright, white hospital room became focused. He blinked, struggling to remember what had happened, but the memories were scattered and fragmented: pain, shining light, and darkness.

When he looked down, he saw the bandages wrapped tightly around his ribs, a dull ache radiating from the wound beneath. He closed his eyes again, trying to piece together the events that had led him here. The last thing he remembered was being out on the street, wandering, high out of his mind. He had been desperate for another hit, drowning himself in drugs to escape the mess that his life had become. And then, there had been someone, an attack. The mugging. His mind flashed to a moment of pain, hands gripping him, and then nothing, just darkness.

He must have passed out, the drugs mixing with the pain, dragging him under. Now, here he was, broken and bruised, lying in a hospital bed with no clear memory of how he had got there.

The door creaked open, and a nurse walked into the room. She was calm, her face a mask of practiced compassion. Alex swallowed, his throat dry, and croaked, "What... happened?"

The nurse glanced at his chart, then back at him, her expression gentle but firm. "You were mugged," she said. "A couple found you unconscious in an alleyway and called 911. You were brought here by ambulance. You're lucky they found you when they did."

Alex let the words sink in, his mind reeling. He didn't feel lucky; he felt hollow, like everything was slipping further and further out of control. He had known he was in a bad place, but lying there in that hospital bed, hearing how close he had come to dying alone in an alley, reality hit him like a tidal wave.

He had been drinking and doing drugs off and on for years, but it had finally caught up with him. His life had spiraled so far out of control that he couldn't even remember how he had ended up on the ground, bleeding and broken. The drugs and alcohol had taken everything from him: his freedom, his relationships, his sense of self. And now, they had nearly taken his life.

The nurse stepped closer, her voice firm but kind. "Alex, you need help. This is your wake-up call. You can't keep going like this. If you do, next time, you might not be so lucky. You need to go to rehab if you want to have any chance of getting better."

Rehab. The word felt heavy, like a burden he wasn't sure he was ready to carry. Alex had heard it before people told him he needed to clean up and get his life together. But he had always shrugged it off, too deep in the fog of addiction to care. But now, lying in that bed, his body aching, the bandages on his ribs a reminder of how far he had fallen, something in him shifted.

He couldn't keep doing this. He couldn't keep running from the pain, hiding behind drugs and alcohol, waiting for the inevitable crash. He had lost everything: his daughter, freedom, and chance at everyday life. But maybe, just maybe, there was still a way out. A way to climb back up, no matter how hard it would be.

Alex swallowed hard, his voice shaky as he looked at the nurse. "I'll go," he said, the words feeling foreign in his mouth. "I'll go to rehab."

The nurse nodded, her eyes softening with relief. "It's a tough road, Alex. But it's the only way forward."

Alex sighed, "I know. I can't keep doing this to myself anymore."

The nurse patted his arm, "You're worth fighting for. You have to believe that."

Alex nodded, "That's the hard part, isn't it?"

Alex lay back on the pillow as she left the room, staring at the ceiling. The path ahead felt daunting, full of uncertainty, full of struggle. But he felt a glimmer of hope for the first time in a long time. He wasn't sure where this journey would lead him, but he knew one thing: he couldn't keep running. He had to face the pain, face the demons he had been trying to outrun for years, and so, with a mix of fear and determination, Alex closed his eyes and prepared himself for the long road to recovery.

July 14th, 2015

Alex sat on the edge of his bed in the rehab facility, staring at the chipped paint on the walls. The air inside felt stifling, thick with the tension of people battling their demons. He had been here for almost a month, and every day felt like a slow grind, an endless loop of the same lectures and routines. The counselors never stopped telling him what to do and how to live his life, like they had it all figured out. They didn't know him. They didn't understand the weight he carried. He was sick of it. It felt like he was back in prison.

He clenched his fists, frustrated by the relentless sense of confinement. He was an adult and didn't need people to tell him how to fix his life. He could do it on his own. That's what he kept telling himself, even as the familiar pull of doubt tugged at the back of his mind.

Across the room, his bunkmate, James, was flipping through a worn-out paperback. James was older, probably in his late forties, with a grizzled face and a quiet demeanor that Alex had come to appreciate. He didn't talk much, but when he did, there was a wisdom to his words that had a way of cutting through the noise. Unlike the counselors, James didn't preach or lecture. He had been through hell and didn't pretend to have all the answers.

"You look like you're ready to bolt," James said suddenly, not looking up from his book.

Alex glanced over, surprised. "I am," he muttered. "I'm done with this place."

James closed the book, setting it down on the bed beside him. "Yeah, I've been there. Feels like they're suffocating you with all their advice, right?"

Alex nodded. "Exactly. They keep telling me how to live but don't know me. They don't know what it's like."

James gave a slight, understanding nod. "You're right they don't. But they've seen enough people like us to know what happens when we don't get our shit together."

Alex bristled at the comment, but James didn't seem to be lecturing him; he spoke from experience. Something about how he said it didn't make Alex feel judged; he just warned.

"I can't stand being told what to do," Alex said, his voice quieter this time. "I've spent my whole life fighting, and I'm tired of being told how I'm supposed to live."

James leaned forward, resting his elbows on his knees, his eyes focused on Alex. "I get that, man. I do. I've been in and out of places like this more than I can count. And each time, I thought I could do it on my own. I thought I didn't need anyone telling me how to fix myself."

Alex looked away, his mind swirling. He had spent so much of his life trying to outrun his past, trying to fix himself, and every time he thought he had a grip on things, they slipped right through his fingers. But the idea of staying here, of listening to people tell him how to be, made his skin crawl.

"I'm leaving," Alex said, more to himself than James.

James sighed, standing up from the bed, walking over to the window, and looking at the rehab grounds. "You can go if you want. No one's stopping you. But before you do, think about what's waiting for you out there."

Alex frowned. "What do you mean?"

"The world won't change just because you leave this place. The streets, the drugs, the people you've run with, they're still out there, waiting for you to slip back in."

Alex knew James was right but didn't want to hear it. He had been out there before, fighting to survive, and he had managed. He could do it again.

James turned to face him, his expression softer now. "I'm not trying to tell you what to do. That's the last thing I want. But I've been where you are, man. I've walked out of places like this thinking I had everything figured out, only to find myself right back where I started."

Alex shifted uncomfortably on the bed, the weight of James's words sinking in. He didn't want to admit it, but a part of him was scared of what might happen if he left, scared that he would fall back into the same patterns and darkness.

"I don't know if I can do this," Alex said quietly, his voice cracking. "What if I can't change?"

James walked back to the bed and sat down across from him. "You can change, Alex. But it's not going to be easy. It never is. The world's not going to hand you anything on a silver platter. You've got to fight for it. And you've got to want it more than you want the escape."

Alex momentarily felt something shift inside him: a flicker of hope and possibility. Maybe James was right. Perhaps this place wasn't just another trap, another prison. Maybe it was a chance, a real chance, to get his life back on track. He had thought about his daughter so many times since rehab began, imagining a future where he could be in her life, be a father to her. Could this be his chance to make that dream a reality? But the pull of the outside world, of freedom, was strong. He had been locked up in one form or another for so long, and the thought of staying here, confined by walls and routines, made his chest tighten.

James must have sensed his inner struggle because he stood up and gave Alex a knowing nod. "It's your decision, man. But before you go, ask yourself: are you running toward or away from something?"

Alex didn't answer. He wasn't sure he knew the answer.

The following day, Alex packed his bags and left rehab, ignoring the counselors' warnings and the uncertainty that gnawed at him. He had made his choice and was determined to prove he could do it on his own.

But as the door to the facility closed behind him, Alex couldn't shake the feeling that he was walking a thin line, teetering on the edge of a dangerous precipice. James's words echoed in his mind, but Alex pushed them away, determined to make it work without anyone's help. He just hoped he was running toward something this time.

August 21st, 2015

Alex had hit rock bottom. There was no more pretending, no more running from the truth. He was homeless and addicted to drugs, and his life was unraveling faster than he could keep up. The streets had become his home, the dark corners of the city his refuge, and each day blurred into the next, a haze of desperation and regret. He had tried to stay afloat, to fight against the current pulling him down, but eventually, he drowned in the habits he thought he could escape, and then, like a miracle he hadn't expected, his old foster father found him.

Alex had been slumped against the side of a building, filthy and too weak to stand, when he heard a familiar voice call his name. At first, he thought he was imagining it, a ghost from his past haunting his ruined life. But when he looked up, there he was, his foster father, standing with a look of disappointment and concern.

Without a word, his foster father bent down and helped Alex to his feet, slipping an arm around his shoulders to support him. The man hadn't aged well; his hair was thinner, his face lined with years of stress, but his strength was still there, and his resolve was as unshakeable as Alex remembered. Together, they returned to the small, modest house Alex had once called home.

Inside, Alex sat on the couch, his body aching, his heart heavy with shame. The warmth of the house was unfamiliar after so many nights in the cold, and the silence between them only made it worse. He didn't know what to say. How do you apologize for falling this far? How do you explain to someone who saved your life once that you've thrown it all away again?

"I don't deserve this," Alex muttered, breaking the silence. His voice was rough, as if the words had been dragged from him.

His foster father sat at the table, his chair creaking as he leaned back, hands folded in front of him. He was quiet for a moment as if considering how to respond. Finally, he spoke, his voice low and steady.

"You deserve a second chance, Alex. We all do. When you came to me when you first got out, I should have done something to help you."

Alex looked up, his eyes stinging with unshed tears. "I don't blame you for not helping me. I've wasted every chance I've had," he said, his voice barely above a whisper. "I've messed up so many times. I don't know how to make it right."

His foster father nodded slowly as if he understood. "Life's full of mistakes. You can't change what's already done, but you can decide what to do next. That's what matters."

Alex swallowed hard, his throat tight. He had heard similar words before, but never like this, never from someone who had always stood by him, even when he didn't deserve it. There was no judgment in his foster father's eyes, no anger—just a quiet belief that maybe, just maybe, Alex could find a way out of the mess he had made.

"I don't know if I can," Alex admitted, his voice cracking. "I don't know if I'm strong enough."

His foster father leaned forward, his gaze steady. "You've survived worse. I've seen you fight back when life tried to beat you down. You've got more strength in you than you think. You have to believe in yourself again."

Alex looked away, the weight of his foster father's words sinking into him. He wasn't sure if he could believe in himself, not after everything he had done, but hearing those words gave him a flicker of hope. It wasn't much, just a tiny, fragile spark, but it was something. And for the first time in a long time, Alex felt like maybe he wasn't entirely alone.

The house was quiet again, the soft ticking of the old wall clock the only sound in the room. Alex sat there, letting the warmth of the moment wash over him. It wasn't redemption, not yet, but it was a start. And as he sat in silence with the man who had never given up on him, Alex allowed himself to hope, just a little, that maybe, this time, he could find a way to make things right.

February 21st, 2016

Alex sat on the porch steps of his foster father's house; the winter air was cool but refreshing. The quiet morning was broken only by the occasional gust of wind, and Alex found comfort in the stillness. Today marked six months of sobriety, a milestone he had never thought he'd reach. It had been six months of battling the cravings, of confronting the demons that had followed him for years. And now, for the first time in a long time, he felt a fragile sense of hope blooming inside him.

He had fought for this moment. The nights of temptation, the constant pull of his past, the urge to numb himself when things got hard, they had all been there, waiting for him to slip. But he hadn't, not this time.

As he sat there, the chip from his recovery meetings resting in his hand, Alex reflected on how far he had come. It hadn't been easy, but he had done it. He was sober, clear-headed, and, for once, proud of himself. He had thought back to all the times he'd tried and failed, how the chaos of his life had always dragged him back down. But this time, he had stayed afloat.

The sound of footsteps pulled him from his thoughts. He looked up to see Daniel, one of the guys from his recovery meetings, walking up the driveway. Daniel was a quiet, usually reserved man, but he had been coming to the same meetings as Alex for months. They didn't talk much, but there was a quiet understanding between them, a bond formed in the shared struggle of addiction.

"Hey, man," Daniel said as he approached, a small smile tugging at the corner of his mouth.

Alex nodded in greeting. "Hey."

Daniel leaned against the porch railing, glancing down at the recovery chip in Alex's hand. "Six months, huh? That's huge."

Alex felt a flicker of pride at Daniel's acknowledgment. "Yeah. I guess it is."

Daniel chuckled softly. "You guess? No, man, it's an accomplishment. Six months is a long time, especially for someone who's been through what you've been through."

Alex looked down at the chip again, running his thumb over its smooth surface. "It hasn't been easy," he admitted. "But I've stuck with it."

"You're stronger than you think, Alex," Daniel said, his voice sincere. "A lot of guys don't make it this far. You've done something real."

For a moment, Alex didn't know how to respond. He had spent many years feeling like a failure, as if every step forward was followed by ten steps back. But hearing someone else acknowledge his progress made something inside him shift. He had come a long way, and maybe, just maybe, he was capable of more than he gave himself credit for.

"I appreciate that," Alex said quietly, looking up at Daniel.

Daniel gave him a nod. "You've earned it."

They stood silently for a moment, the weight of Daniel's words sinking in. Alex wasn't used to hearing praise, especially not for something as personal and complex as sobriety. But in that moment, it felt natural. It felt like he had accomplished something important, something worth holding on to.

As Daniel pushed off the railing and turned to leave, he paused, glancing back at Alex. "You keep going, all right? No matter what. You've got something to fight for; don't forget that."

Alex nodded, his throat tight with emotion. "I won't."

When Daniel left, Alex sat there longer, the recovery chip still resting in his hand. It felt different now, heavier, more meaningful. For the first time, he allowed himself to believe that he was on the right path, that maybe he really could make a life for himself beyond addiction. The idea of his daughter flashed briefly through his mind, and he wondered if there was still a chance to build some connection with her one day.

The road ahead was still long, and there would be challenges. Alex knew that. But for the first time in years, he felt like he wasn't just surviving; he was moving forward. He was making progress, and that was enough to keep him going.

May 3rd, 2016

Alex sat in his room, the silence pressing around him like a heavyweight. His foster father was his anchor, and his guide was gone. Just like that, with no warning, no chance to say goodbye. A massive heart attack had taken him, leaving Alex feeling as though the ground had been ripped out from under him.

The man who had stood by him through some of the darkest moments of his life was gone, just like everyone else. It felt like a cruel pattern, a life where those he cared about were always taken away too soon, leaving him to pick up the pieces alone. Alex had already lost his parents, and his daughter felt like a distant dream. The man who had given him a second chance when he didn't deserve one was gone, too.

Alex stared blankly at the wall, his thoughts swirling in a fog of grief and uncertainty. What was he supposed to do now? His foster father had been more than just someone who took him in; he had been a father figure, a mentor, the one person who had always believed in him when Alex couldn't even believe in himself. The man who had helped him get sober, who had taken him in when he was homeless and lost, had been a constant presence in his life when everything else had fallen apart, and now, he was gone.

The funeral had been small, with a few friends and distant relatives, but the emptiness left behind felt vast, like a void Alex couldn't fill. He had been through so much with his foster father the years of tough love, the lessons, the unspoken understanding between them, and now there was nothing but the hollow ache of loss.

Alex wiped his face with his hand, but the tears wouldn't stop. He had never been good at dealing with grief, always turning to drugs or alcohol to numb the pain. But this time, he was determined to stay sober. It was what his foster father would have wanted. But that resolve didn't make the pain any less suffocating.

The house felt too quiet, too still, without his foster father's presence moving through the rooms. Alex could hear the echo of their conversations in his mind, the advice, the gentle reprimands, the moments of silence when no words were needed. Now, all of it was just a memory, a painful reminder of what he had lost.

As he sat in the darkened room, Alex wondered what his next step was. He had been leaning on his foster father for support, and without him, the path forward felt uncertain and terrifying. He knew he had to figure out what to do, but right now, it felt impossible. The weight of loss was too fresh, too heavy.

Deep down, Alex also knew that his foster father would want him to keep going. He would like Alex to stay strong, to continue the path of sobriety, and to find a way to build a life, even in the face of grief.

Still, as Alex sat in his room, mourning the loss of the man who had saved him more times than he could count, he couldn't help but feel lost. The grief was overwhelming, and all he could do was sit there and let it wash over him, knowing that, once again, he was left to face the world without the person he had depended on the most.

May 15th, 2016

Alex sat motionless in the corner of the small room, his back against the cold wall, the phone still clutched in his trembling hand. The voice on the other end of the line had delivered the words, but they didn't feel real. Kate and his daughter Hannah were dead. They had been killed in a car accident by a drunk driver. The finality was too much to process, too cruel to believe. It felt like a bad dream, one he kept waiting to wake from, but the reality was sinking in, slowly and painfully. His daughter was gone.

Alex's mind raced, fragments of memories and hopes colliding in a haze of grief. He hadn't been there for her. He had missed her entire childhood. But he had always held on to the hope that one day, somehow, they would find each other, and he would finally be the father she deserved. Now, that hope had been snatched away, leaving nothing but an emptiness he had no idea how to fill.

He dropped the phone onto the floor, the clattering sound barely registering in his fog of despair. His hands gripped the edge of the bed, knuckles white, as if holding on might keep him from drowning in the overwhelming tide of sorrow. His chest ached with its weight, his breath coming in shallow, uneven gasps.

For a long time, he just sat there, letting the grief wash over him, letting it consume him. But then, as the tears subsided, something else flickered at the edges of his consciousness, something faint but unmistakable.

A thought. A question. What if this isn't the end? Alex lifted his head slowly, his eyes landing on the small photo of his daughter that he kept beside the bed, which Kate had sent him two years ago. He reached for it, his fingers brushing the worn edges of the picture. His daughter's bright, smiling face stared back at him, full of life and possibility. She had been so beautiful, so full of promise. And even though he had never met her, she had been the one thing in his life that had kept him going, the one dream he had never let go of.

His mind raced with conflicting thoughts, the grief battling with a fragile sense of determination. He had spent years trapped in a cycle of pain and regret, trying to outrun his past, only to be pulled back in repeatedly. But maybe... just maybe... this didn't have to be the end of the line. Perhaps this could be the turning point—the moment he made a different choice and decided to fight, not for his daughter's sake, but for his own.

Alex felt his heart pound harder, the weight of the loss still pressing down on him, but alongside it, something else was stirring, a flicker of light in the darkness. He thought about the meetings he had attended, the people he had met who had been through hell and back and somehow managed to keep going. He had seen men who had lost everything yet still found a way to rebuild. He had seen the possibility of redemption, even in despair. What if he could find that too?

His eyes moved from the photo to his phone lying on the floor. He could call his sponsor. He could reach out for help. He could attend a meeting tonight. It wasn't too late. There was still time to turn things around and fight for the future he had always wanted. Even though the road ahead seemed impossibly long and challenging, wasn't it worth trying?

His hand trembled as he picked up the phone, his heart racing uncertainly. He stared at the screen for an eternity, his thumb hovering over the contact list. He knew what he had to do; he had known for a long time, but the weight of it all felt so heavy.

As Alex sat there, holding the phone in his hand, something inside him shifted. He thought about his daughter again, about what she might have wanted for him. She had never known him, but if she had, wouldn't she have wanted him to fight? To keep going? To try to live a life he could be proud of?

A tear slid down Alex's cheek, but this time, it wasn't from despair; it was from something deeper, something more hopeful. He felt he had a choice for the first time in a long time. He took a deep breath and pressed the button.

The phone rang.

Epilogue

The room was quiet, save for the faint, uneven creak of a chair rocking gently against the floor. Alex stood by the window, staring at the fading light of dusk, the weight of everything pressing down on him. In one hand, he held his phone; in the other, the frayed rope he had taken out earlier that day. His fingers traced the coarse fibers as his thumb hovered over the screen. He had tried calling once or twice earlier, but the calls went straight to voicemail.

Maybe they're busy, he had thought. *Perhaps they'll call back.*

But the silence was deafening, and now, as the light outside began to fade, Alex's patience was wearing thin. The phone felt heavy in his hand, like a last tether to the world he was trying to stay connected to, but that world felt so far away. His legs trembled slightly, and sweat beaded on his forehead, not from fear but from the terrible certainty of what he was about to do.

He sat down on the chair, laying the phone beside him, and began tying the rope with trembling hands. He had researched it all—how to tie the knot, ensure the drop was quick, and that there would be no mistakes. *No more mistakes*. His life had been nothing but a long string of them, and now, he was determined to get this one thing right.

A small voice inside him still urged him to try one last time. To call someone, anyone.

With the noose hanging above him, Alex again reached for the phone. He scrolled through his contacts, pausing on the name of his sponsor. He pressed the call button and listened to the ringing. His heart raced in his chest, a quiet part of him hoping to hear a voice on the other end. The ringing stopped.

Voicemail.

Alex exhaled slowly, a sense of resignation settling over him. He left no message. He hung up.

His fingers trembled as he scrolled to the next number. Another person from the meetings. He pressed the call button, his breath catching as it rang. And rang. His pulse quickened, a part of him desperate for anyone to answer. But then, the familiar beep of voicemail again. No one was there.

A lump formed in his throat, and he lowered the phone, staring at the screen. He wiped the sweat from his brow, setting the phone on the table beside him. He glanced at the rope hanging above the foyer, tight and secure knots. He had done everything right this time, and there would be no mistake.

Still, the voice inside him whispered, urging him to try again. With shaking hands, Alex picked up the phone once more. He found a third name he had known from his old life. Someone who had told him once, years ago, that if he ever needed help, they would be there. Alex hit call, his thumb pressing down harder than required, almost willing them to pick up. The phone rang. His heart pounded as it rang again and again.

Voicemail.

Alex stared at the phone, his breath coming in ragged gasps now. He let the phone drop from his hand, falling onto the floor beside him. The screen was still illuminated with the missed call. It was over. No one was coming.

He stood up, the room spinning slightly as he positioned the chair beneath the noose. The wood creaked under his weight as he stepped up, the rope swaying gently from the ceiling. His hands were steady now, his movements slow and deliberate as he placed the noose around his neck, tightening it as he had practiced, making sure everything was just right.

For a moment, Alex hesitated. He looked down at the phone one last time, hoping, wishing for it to ring. For someone to call back and pull him out of this. But the screen stayed dark.

He closed his eyes, feeling the rough texture of the rope pressing into his skin, his heart pounding in his chest. The chair's creak was the only sound now, faint and rhythmic, as Alex took a deep breath. He was ready.

He exhaled slowly, closing his eyes, the tension in his chest loosening as he accepted what was coming. It was time. There was no turning back now.

With a final, deliberate movement, Alex stepped off the chair and over the railing. Gravity took hold, and he fell six feet in an instant. The rope jerked violently as the slack ran out, and he felt the noose tighten around his neck, the sudden, crushing pressure cutting off his breath. His body jolted as the sharp crack of his neck echoed through his skull, a brief flare of pain exploding in his mind. Then, it was over. The pain disappeared as quickly as it had come, replaced by a strange, weightless numbness. His body dangled four feet above the floor, swaying gently from the rope, life draining from him as the final moments of his existence played out in the recesses of his dying mind.

Memories flashed before him, flickers of the people he loved, his choices, and the life he had tried and failed to live. The weight of those memories, once unbearable, now seemed to fade, becoming distant and blurred as the world slipped further and further away. Then there was nothing.

Alex's limp body swayed slightly in the fading light of the day. The house was silent again, the chair lying on its side, unmoving.

Author's Note:

Dear Reader,

By the time you've reached the end of this story, you may find yourself grappling with the weight of its conclusion. Alex's journey, from childhood to his final moments, was marked by pain, addiction, loss, and moments of fleeting hope. I chose to end his story with darkness not to glorify despair but to reflect the reality of what so many people face in the shadows of their lives. The truth is, for some, the weight of trauma and addiction becomes overwhelming, and the path to redemption is not always clear or specific.

This story was written to honor those struggling daily with these invisible battles. The darkness in the ending reflects the harsh truth that not everyone finds a way out. But in sharing Alex's story, I hope to encourage conversations about the importance of mental health, addiction recovery, and desperately needed support systems.

However, the dark ending does not mean that hope is absent. Life is complicated, and though Alex's journey ended in tragedy, I believe that for many others, the ending can be different. I want to remind you that no matter how difficult life becomes, there is always a path forward, even when it seems impossible. Help is out there, sometimes in the form of friends, family, or professionals, and sometimes in unexpected places.

If you or someone you know is struggling, I urge you to reach out. There is light, even when it feels hidden by the shadows.

Thank you for taking the time to read this story. I hope it resonates with you through understanding, empathy, or a call to action. We must be there for each other, especially when the darkness overwhelms us.

With hope,

Brandon Michaels

www.ingramcontent.com/pod-product-compliance
Lightning Source LLC
Chambersburg PA
CBHW031605240626
47153CB00002B/641